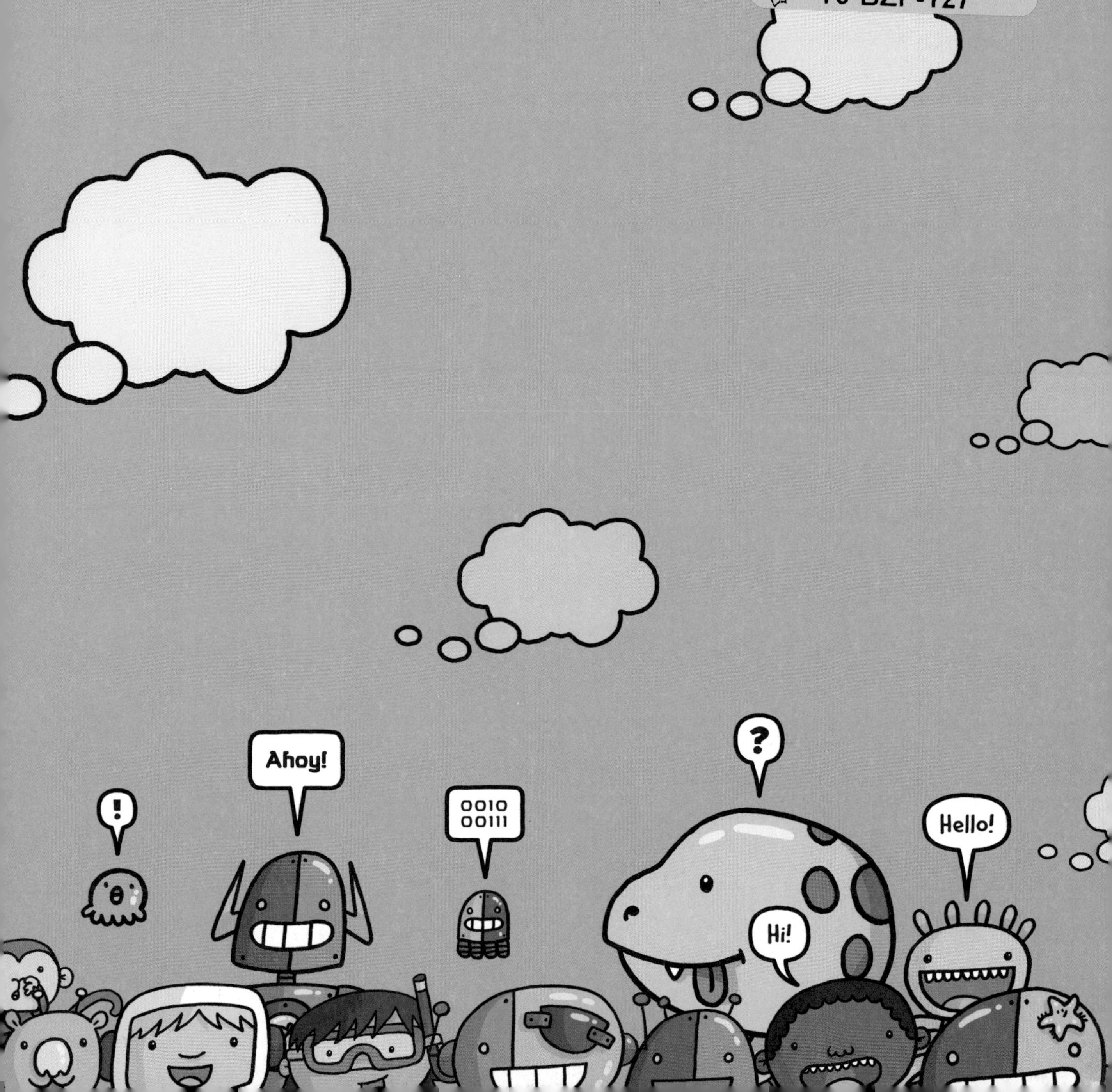
!
Ahoy!
0010
00111
?
Hi!
Hello!

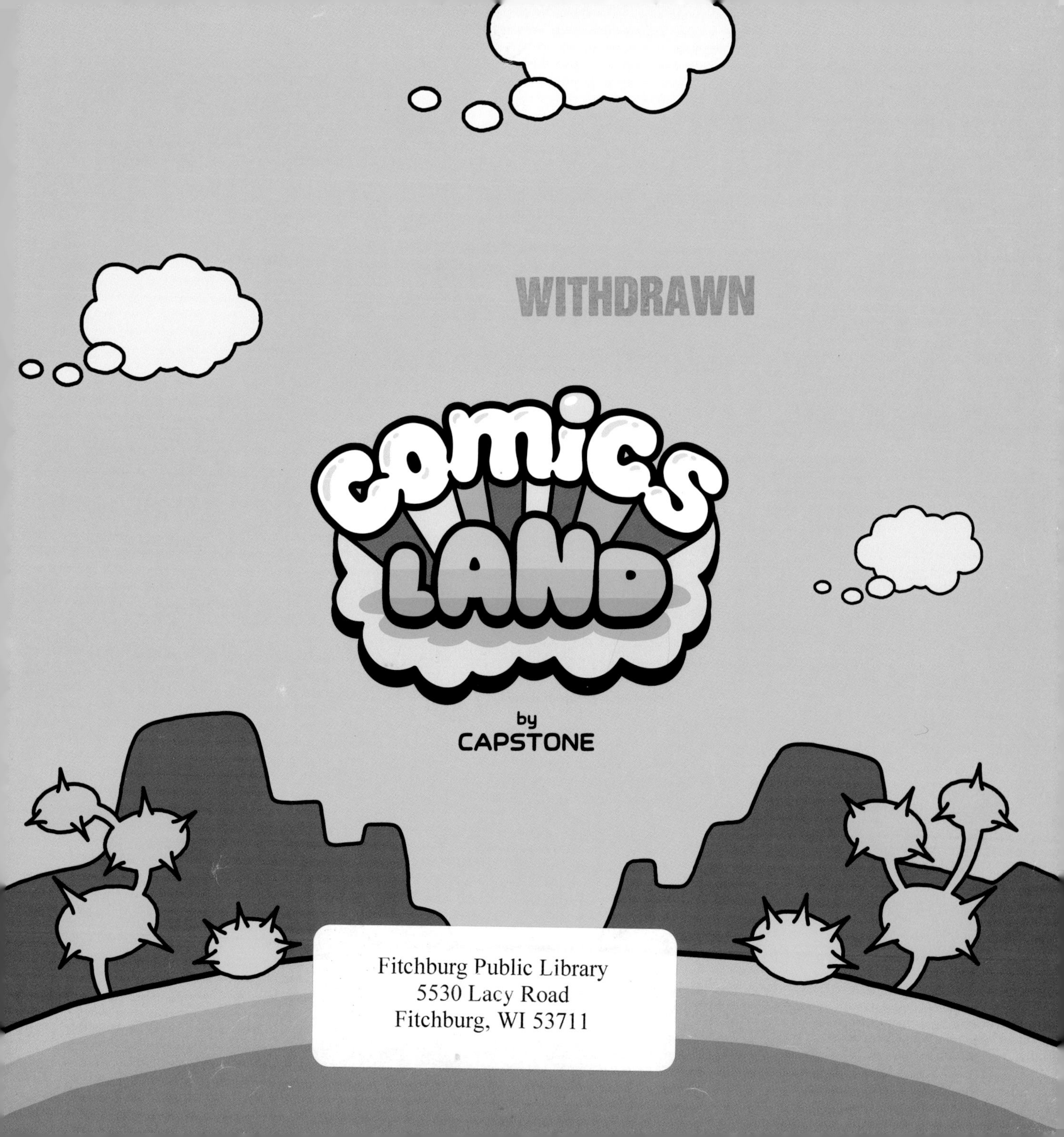
COMICS LAND
by
CAPSTONE

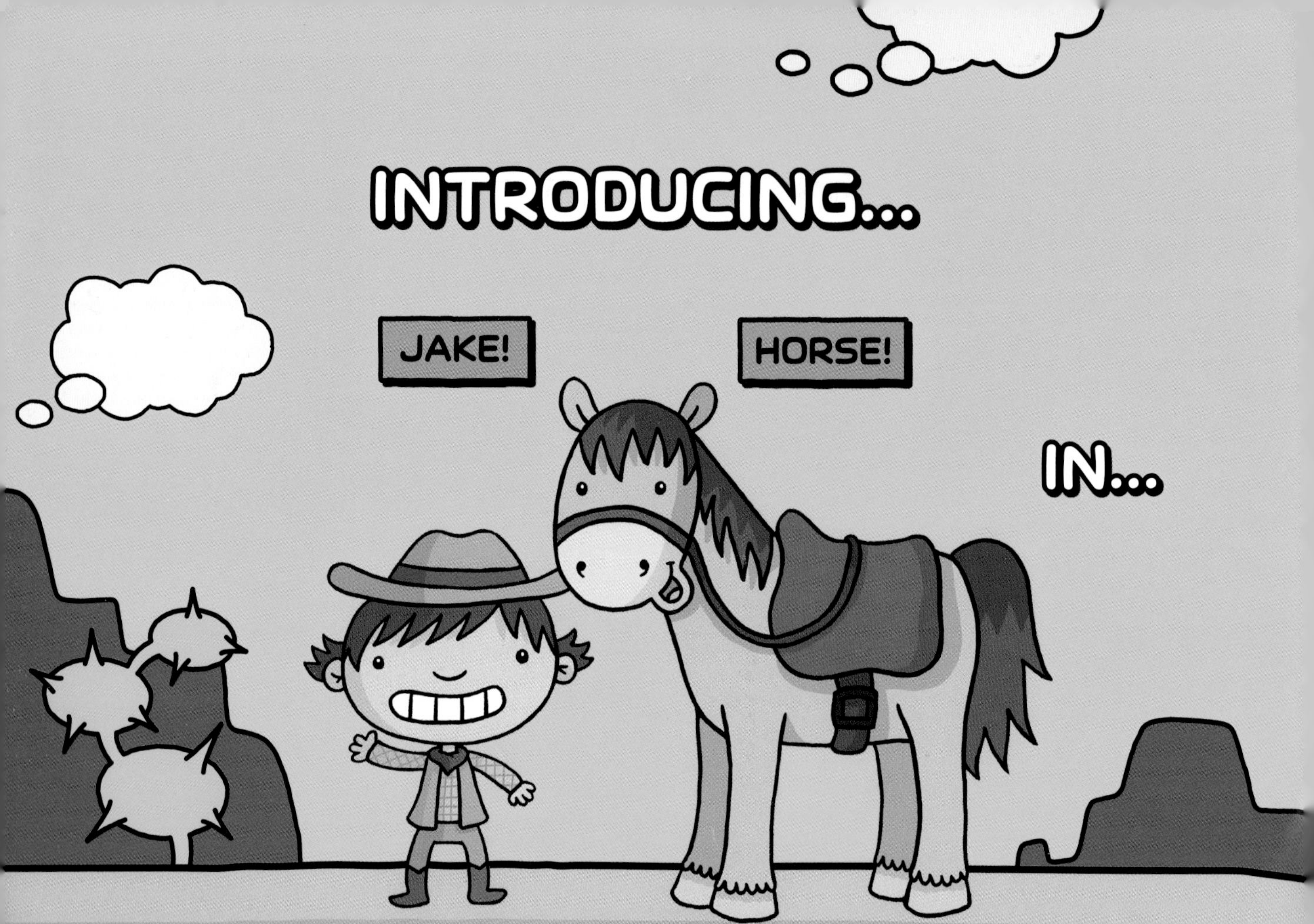
INTRODUCING...
JAKE!
HORSE!
IN...

capstone
www.capstoneyoungreaders.com

1710 Roe Crest Drive, North Mankato, Minnesota 56003

Cataloging-in-Publication data is available on the Library of Congress website.
ISBN: 978-1-4342-6283-7 (hardcover) • ISBN: 978-1-4342-4945-6 (library binding) •
ISBN: 978-1-4342-6430-5 (eBook)

Printed in China by Nordica. 0413/CA21300502 032013 007226NORDF13

THE GOOD, THE BAD, AND THE MONKEYS

written by
SCOTT SONNEBORN

illustrated by
JESS BRADLEY

designed by
BOB LENTZ

edited by
JULIE GASSMAN

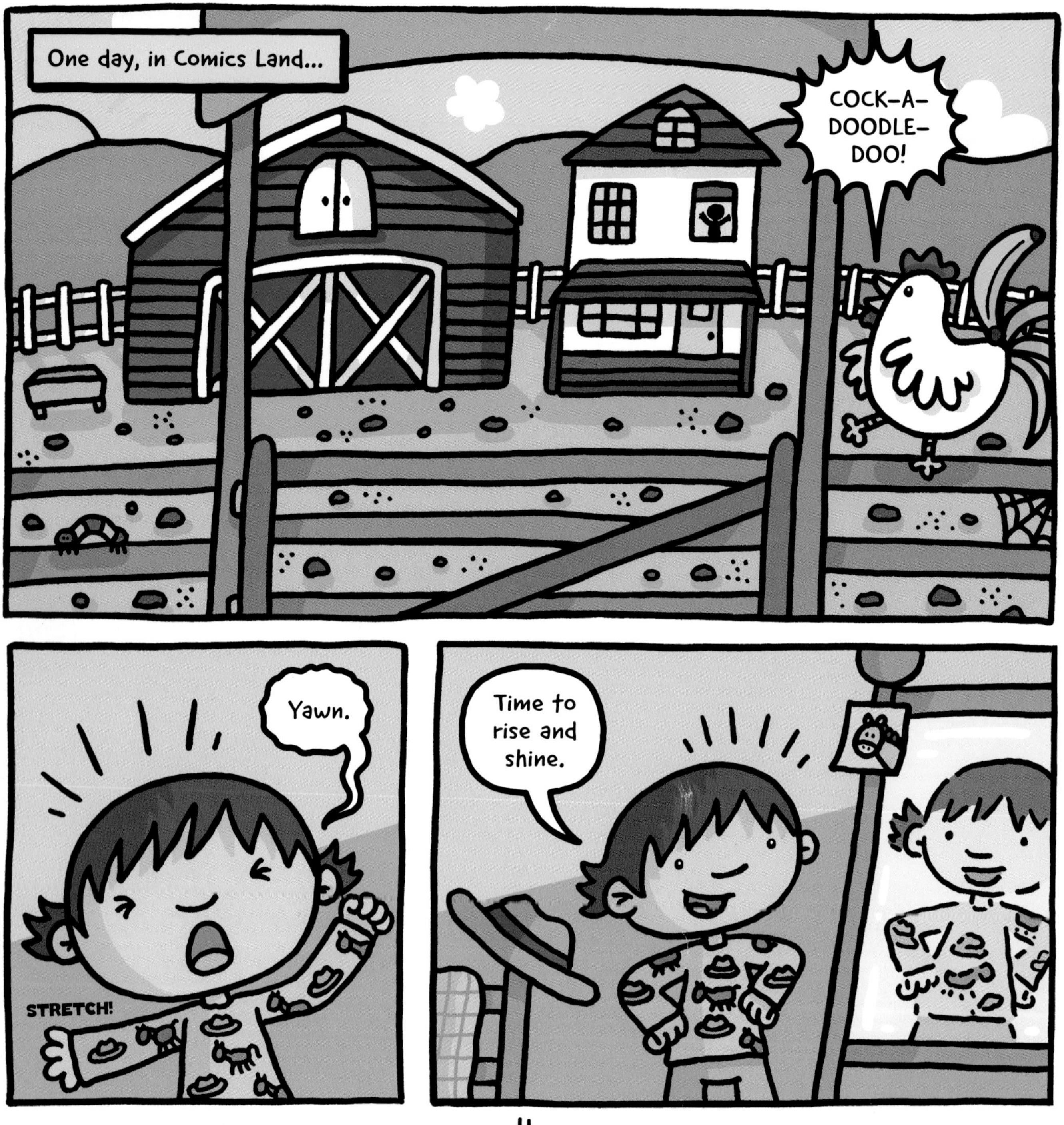
One day, in Comics Land...
COCK-A-DOODLE-DOO!
Yawn.
STRETCH!
Time to rise and shine.

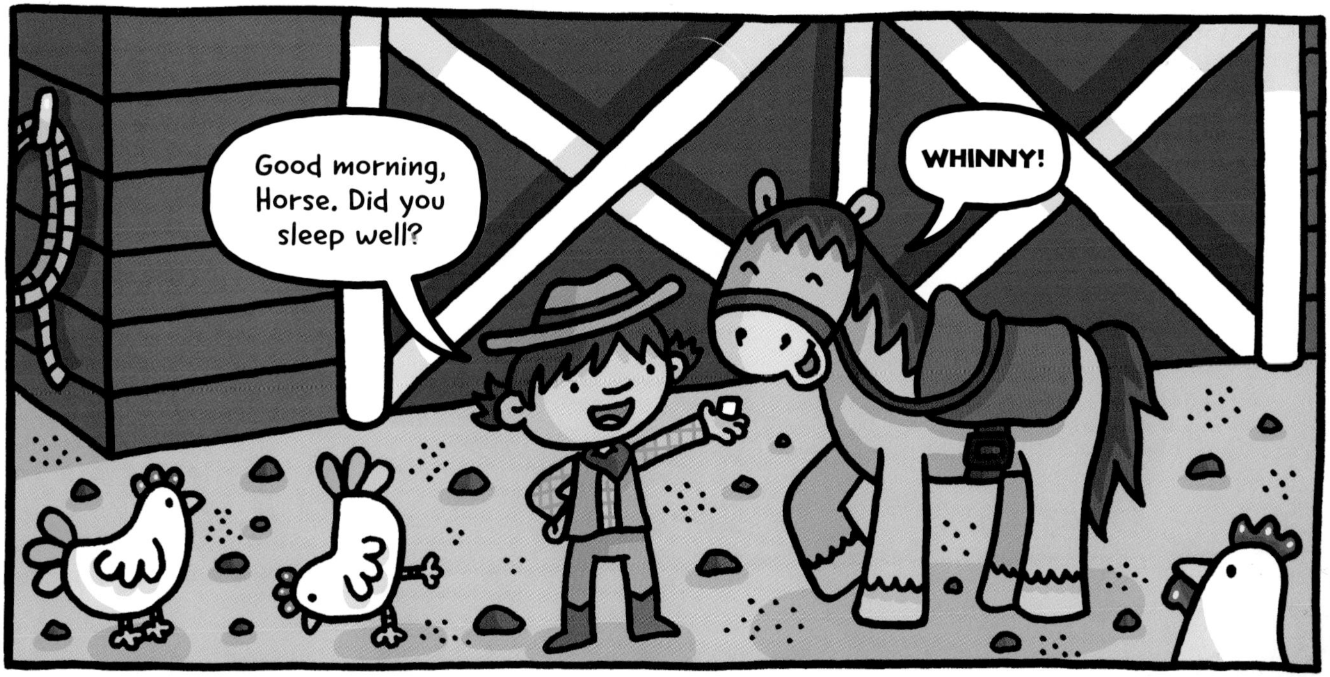
Good morning, Horse. Did you sleep well?
WHINNY!

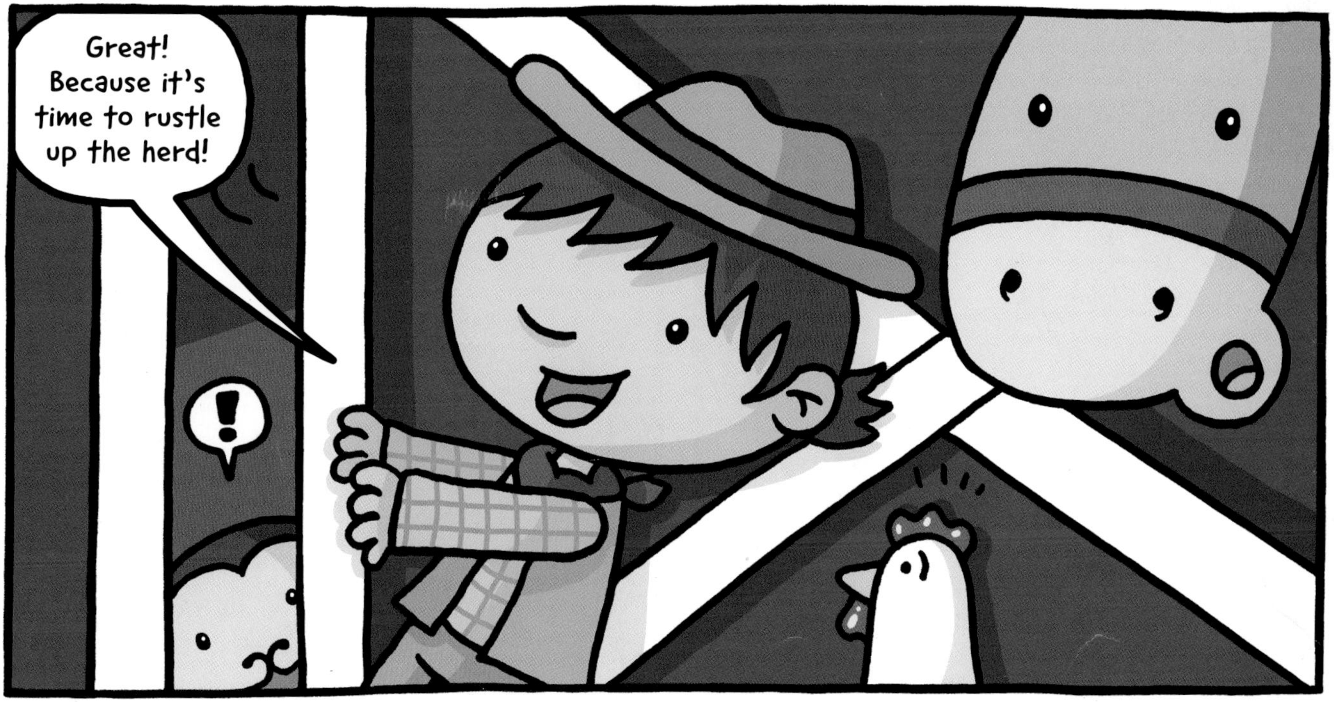
Great! Because it's time to rustle up the herd!
!

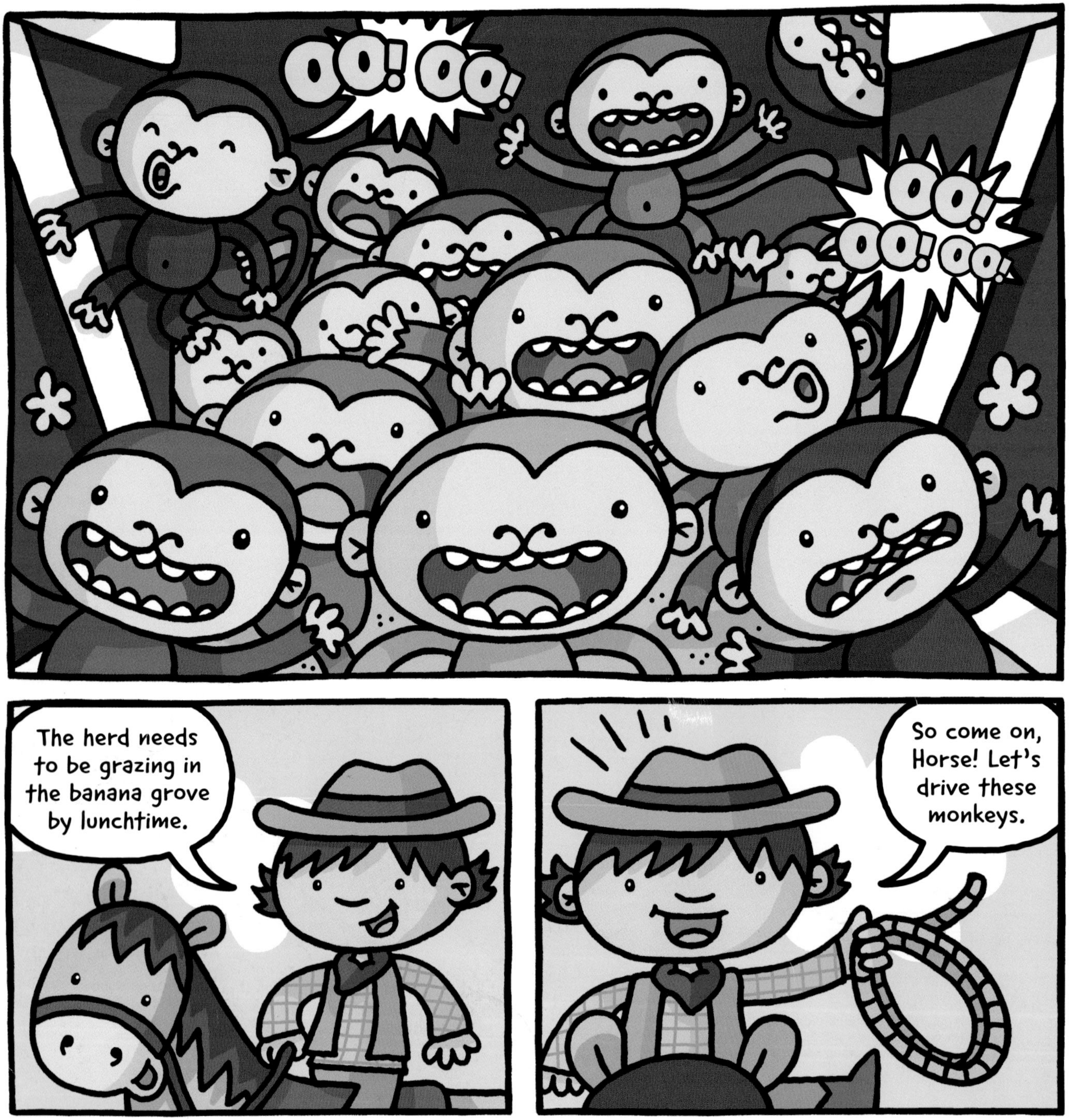
OO! OO!
OO! OO! OO!
The herd needs to be grazing in the banana grove by lunchtime.
So come on, Horse! Let's drive these monkeys.

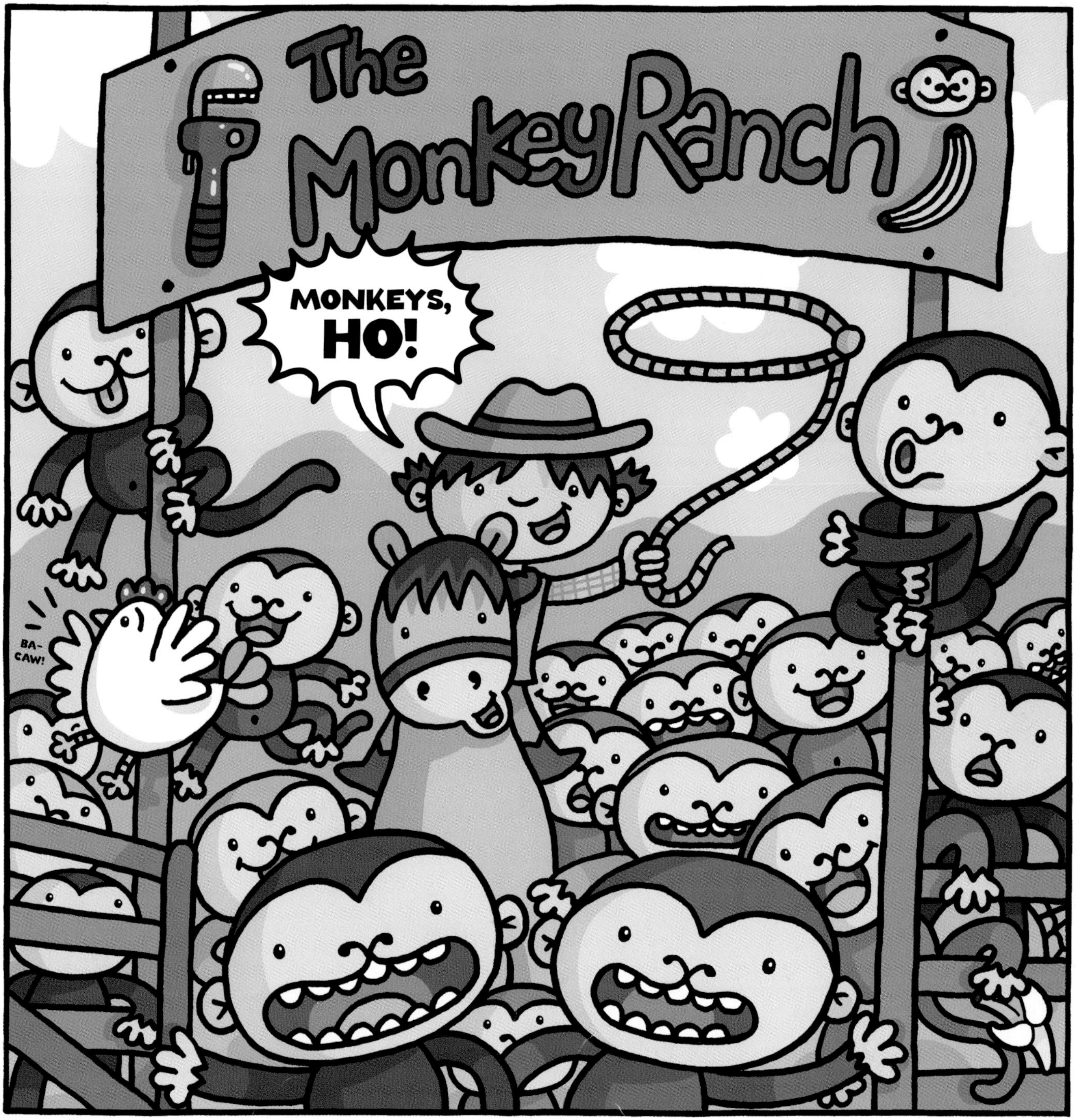
The MonkeyRanch
MONKEYS, HO!
BA-CAW!

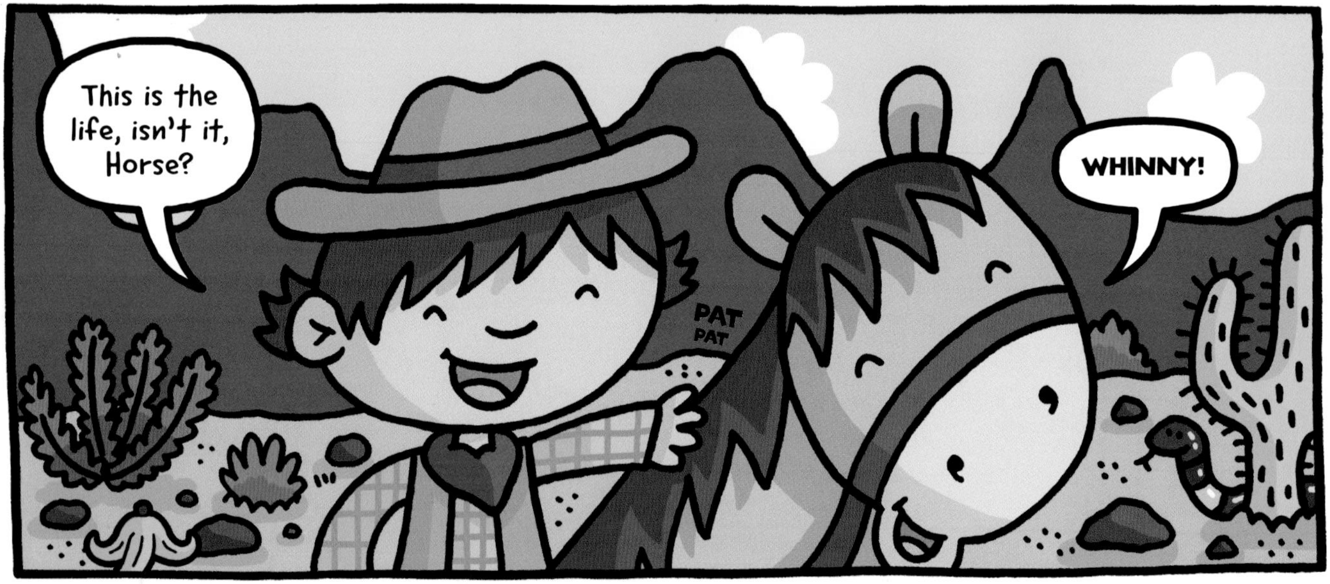
This is the life, isn't it, Horse?
PAT PAT
WHINNY!

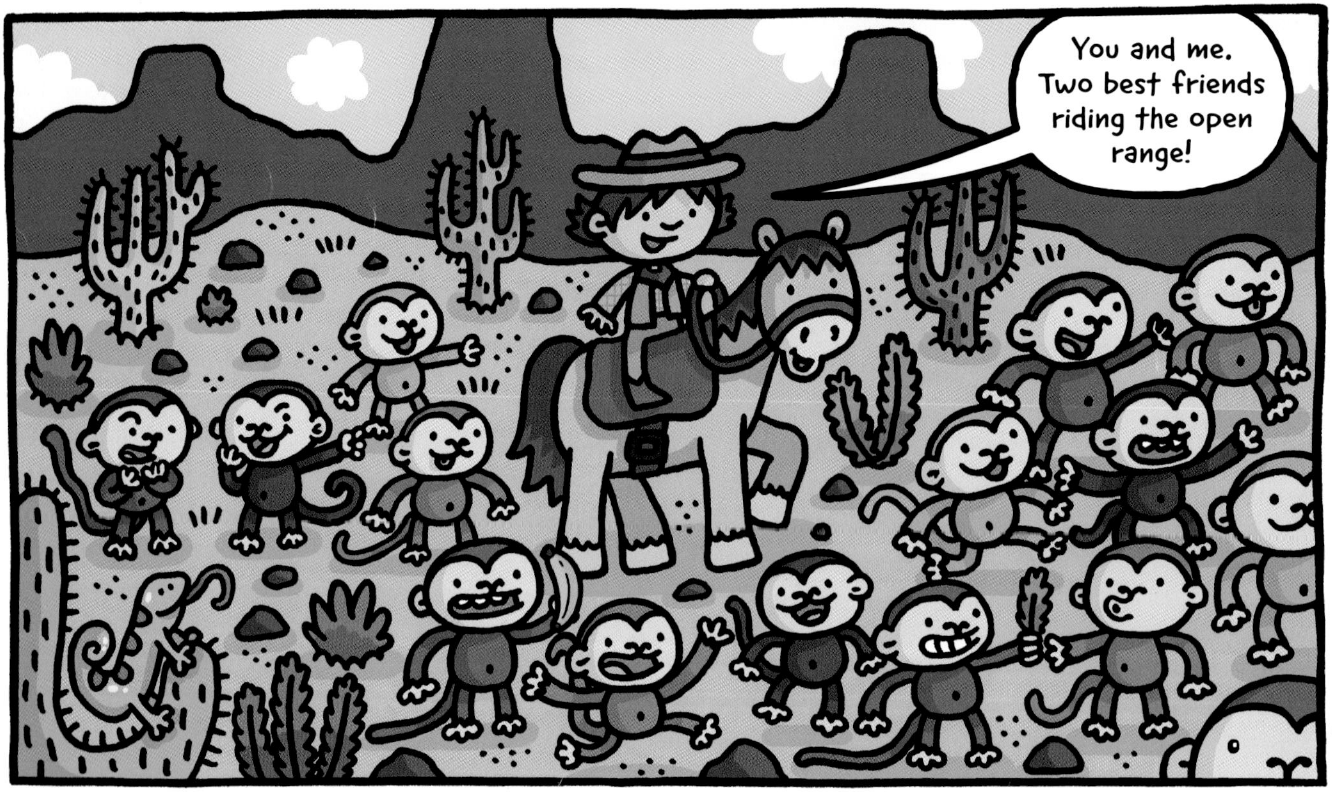
You and me. Two best friends riding the open range!

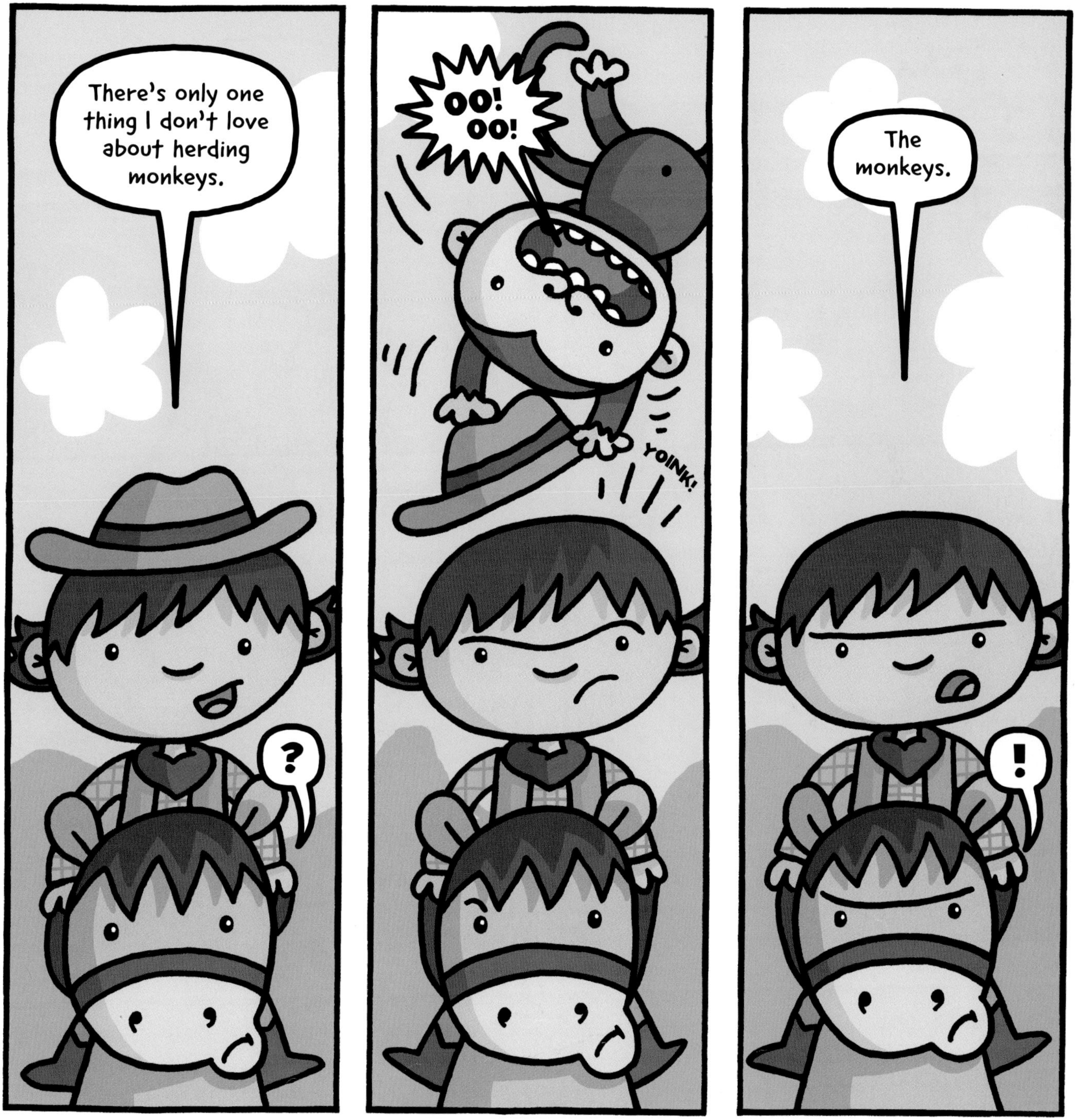
There's only one thing I don't love about herding monkeys.
?
OO! OO!
YOINK!
The monkeys.
!

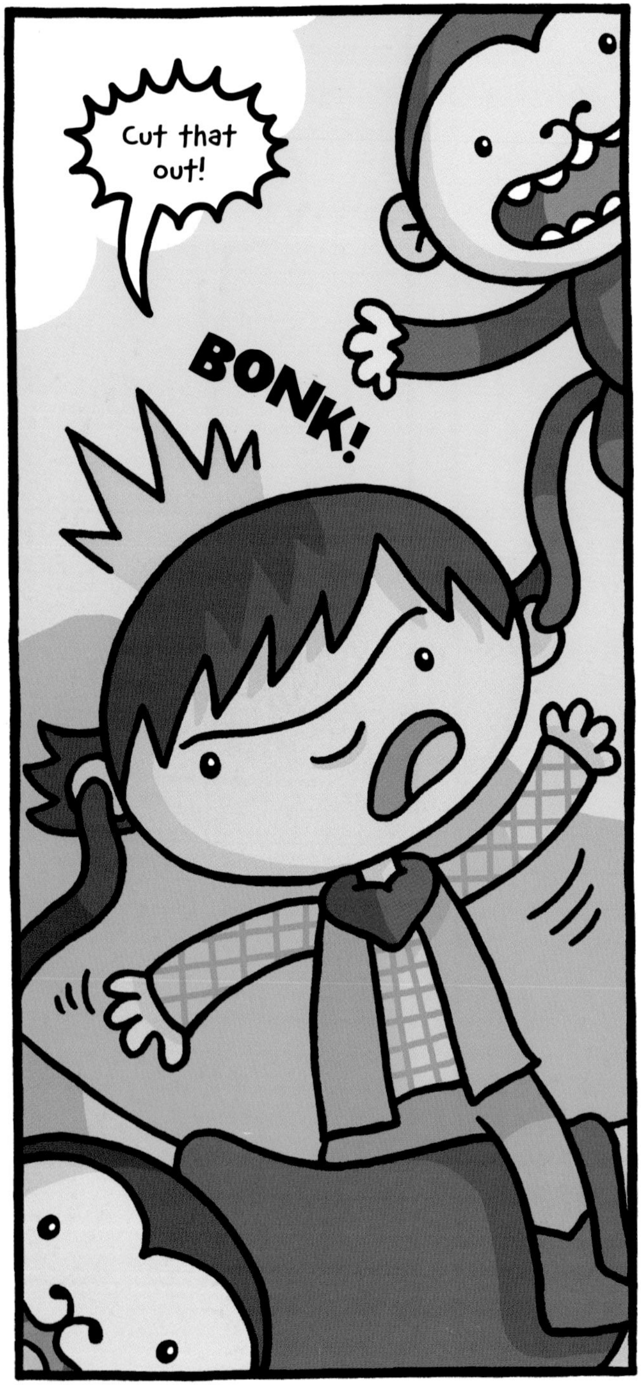
Cut that out!
BONK!

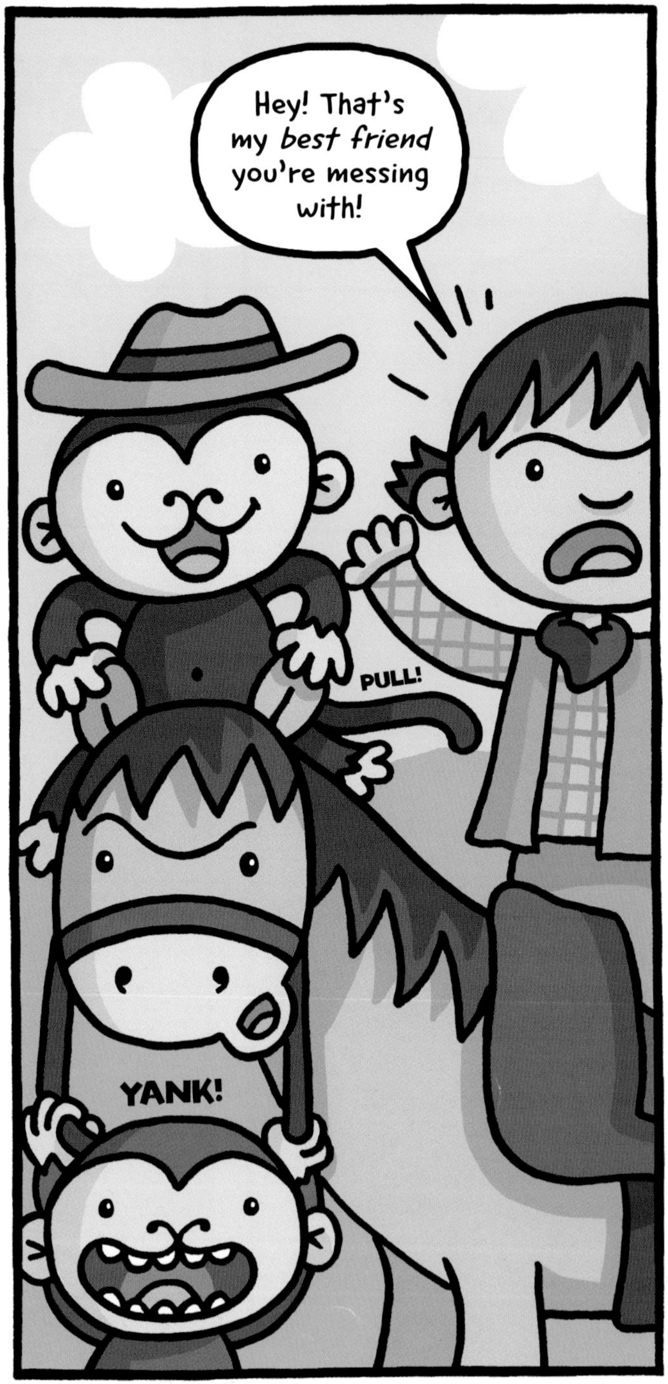
Hey! That's my *best friend* you're messing with!
PULL!
YANK!

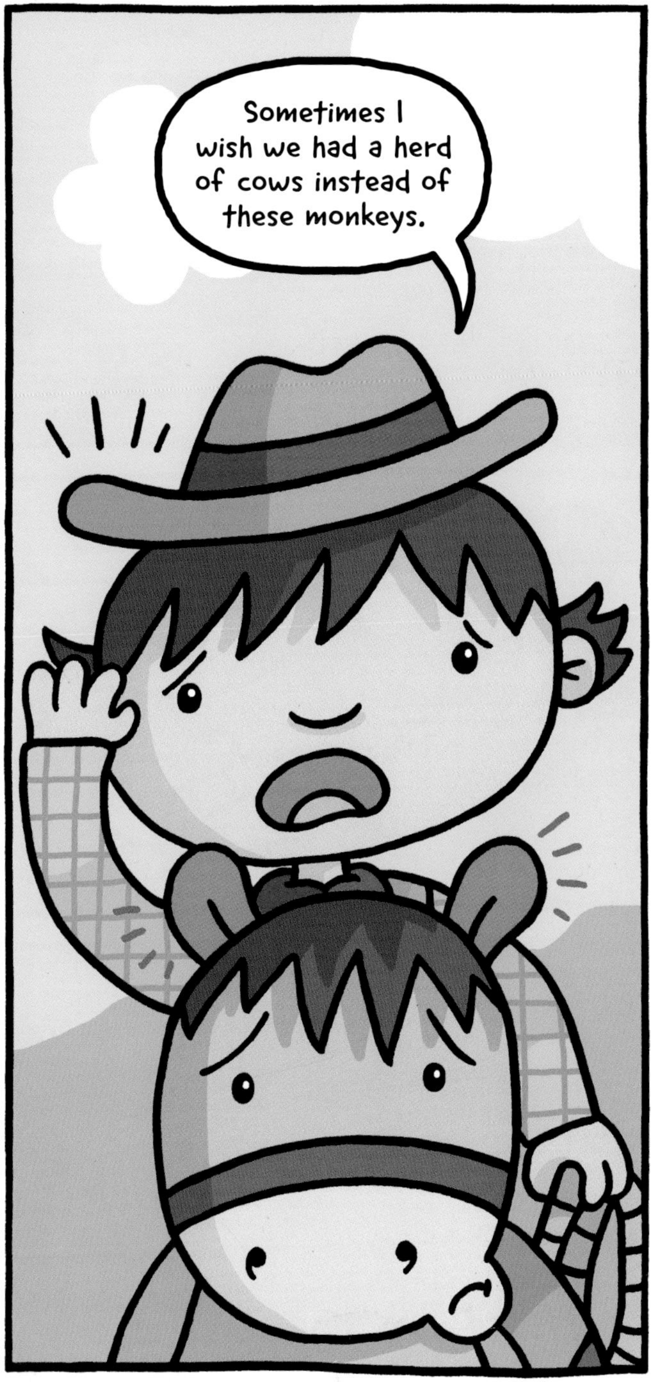
Sometimes I wish we had a herd of cows instead of these monkeys.

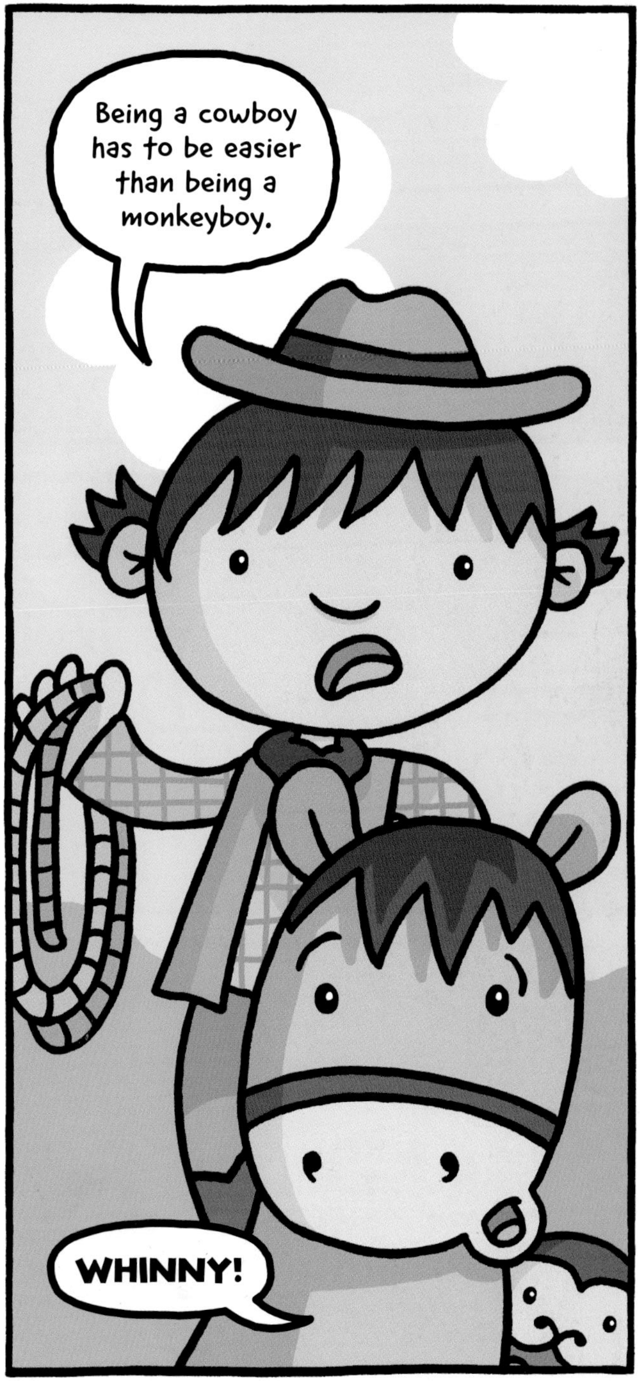
Being a cowboy has to be easier than being a monkeyboy.
WHINNY!

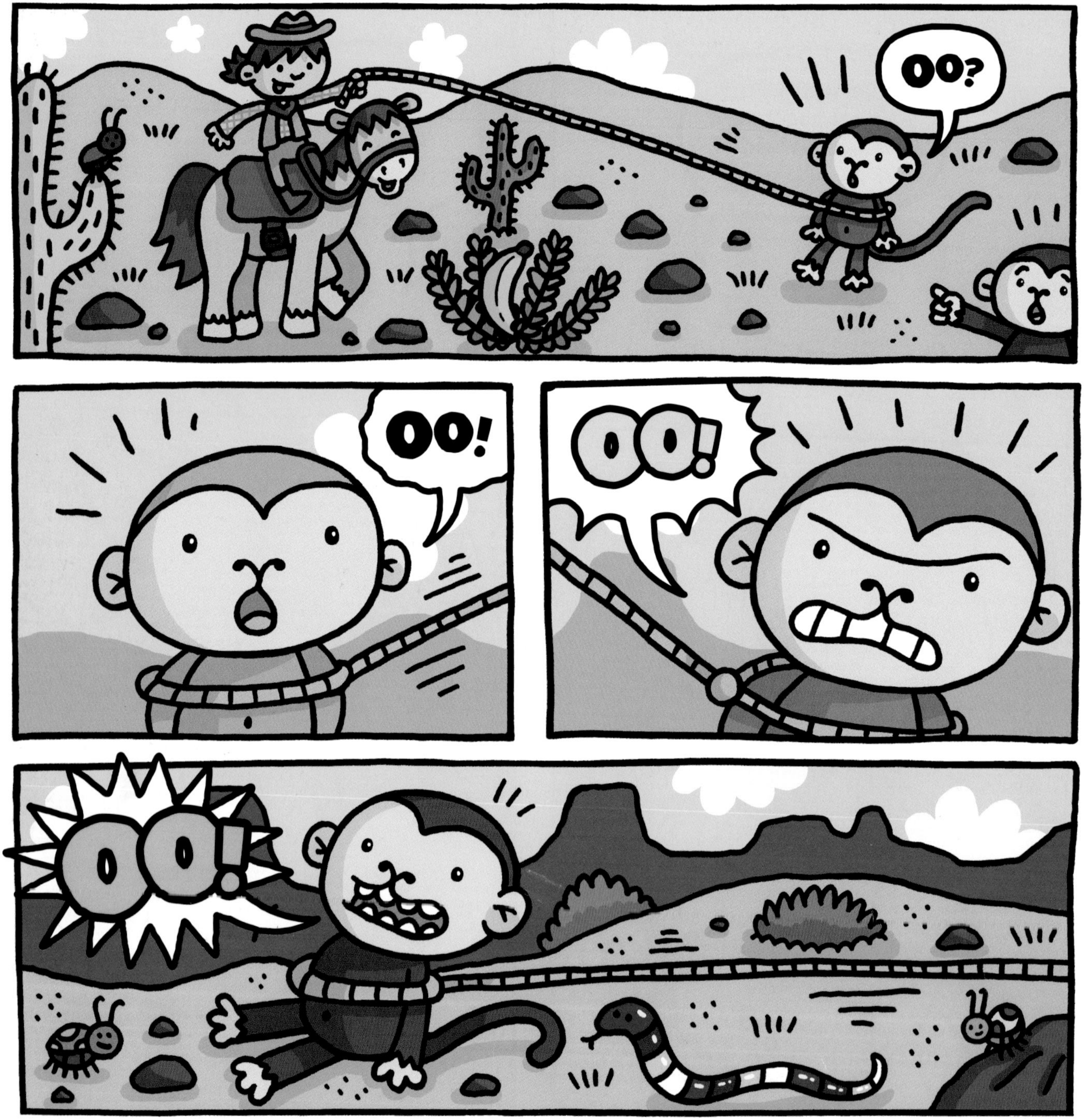
OO?
OO!
OO!
OO!

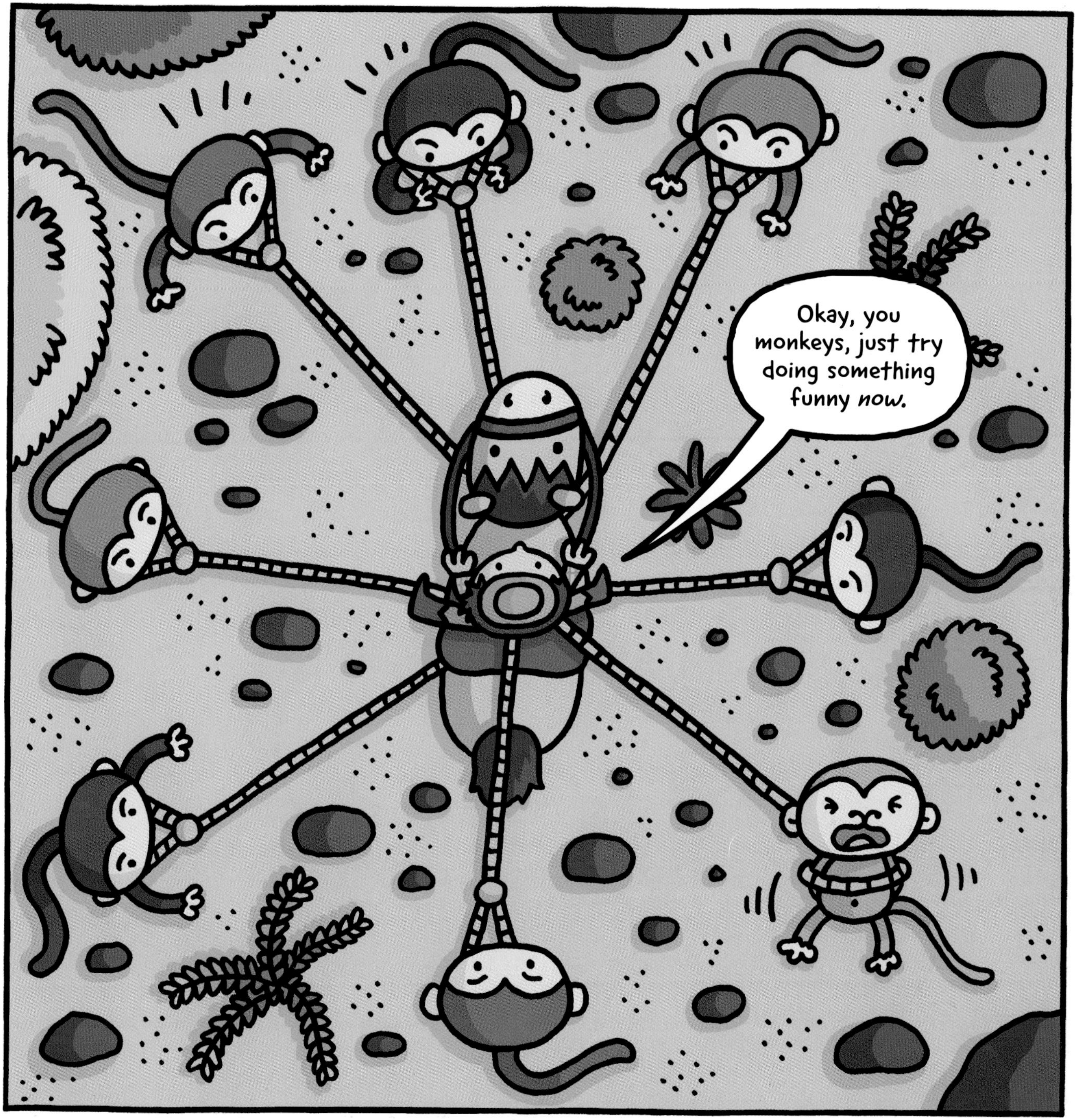
Okay, you monkeys, just try doing something funny *now*.

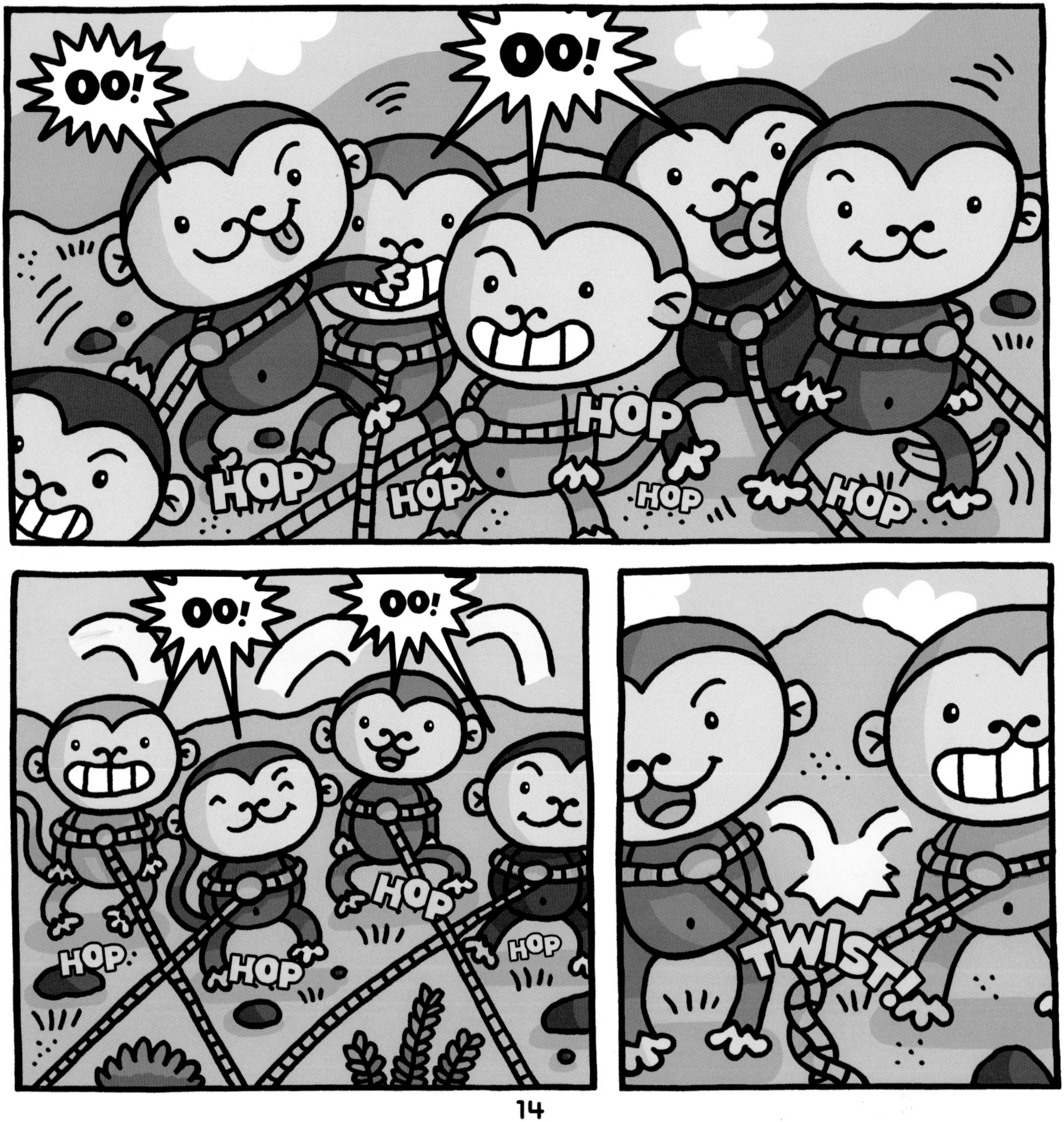

OO!
OO!
HOP
HOP
HOP
HOP
HOP
OO!
OO!
HOP
HOP
HOP
HOP
TWIST!

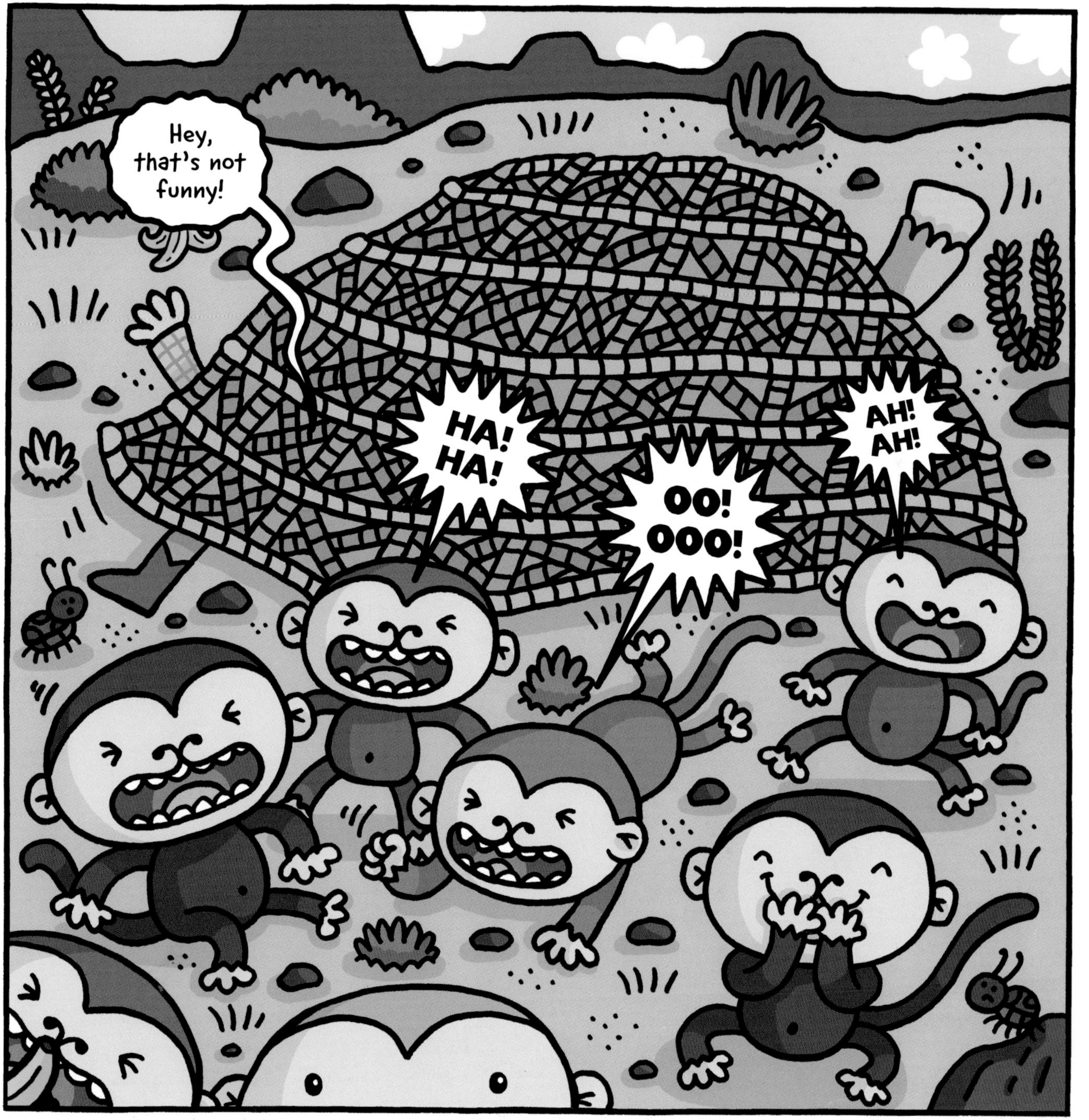

Hey, that's not funny!
HA! HA!
OO! OOO!
AH! AH!

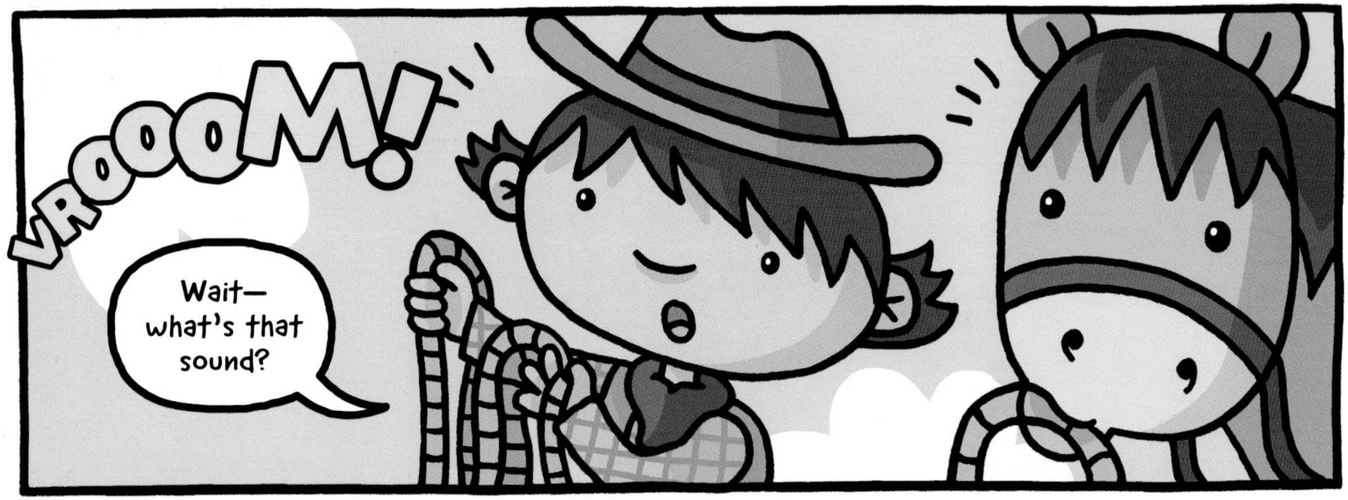
VROOOM!
Wait— what's that sound?

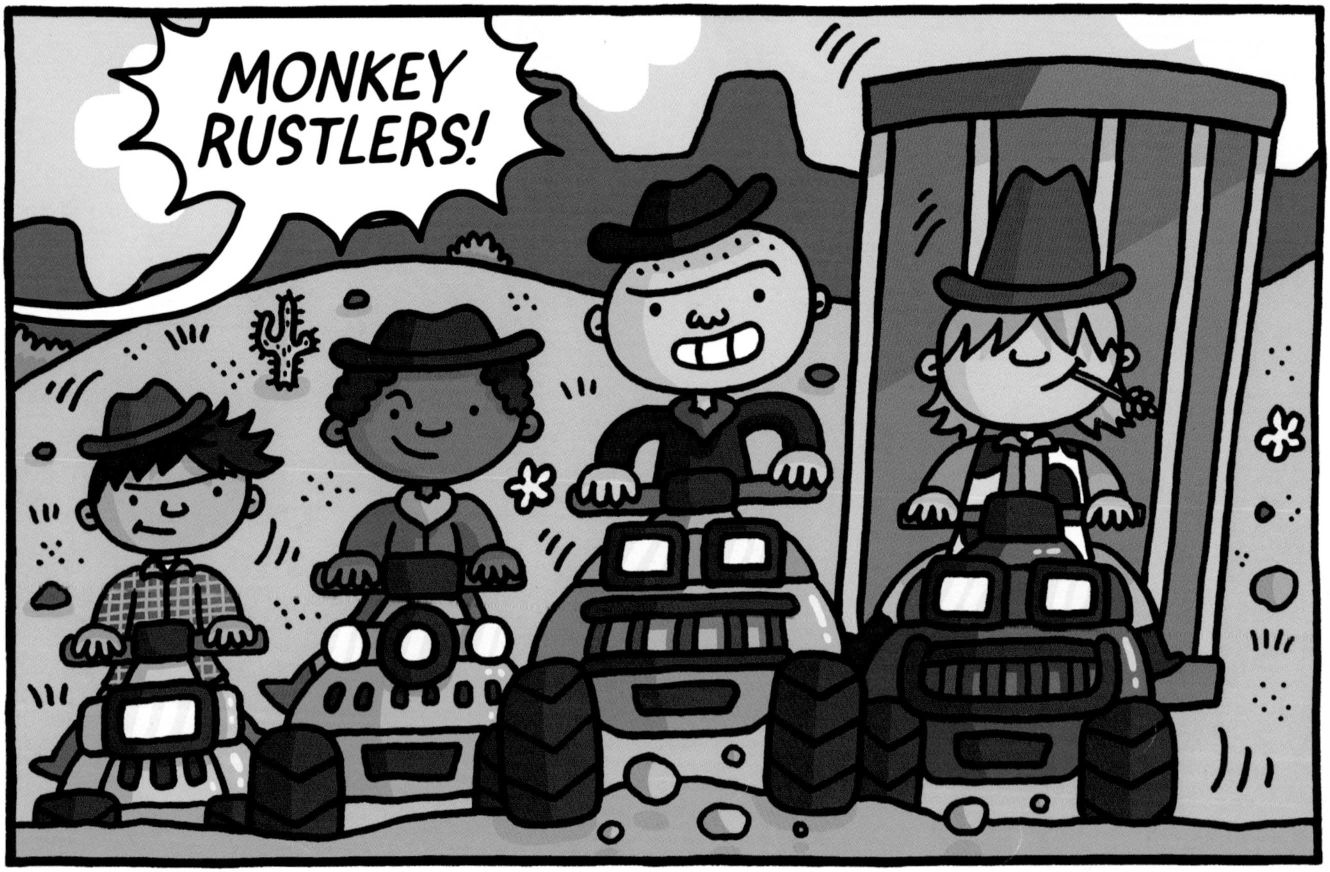
MONKEY RUSTLERS!

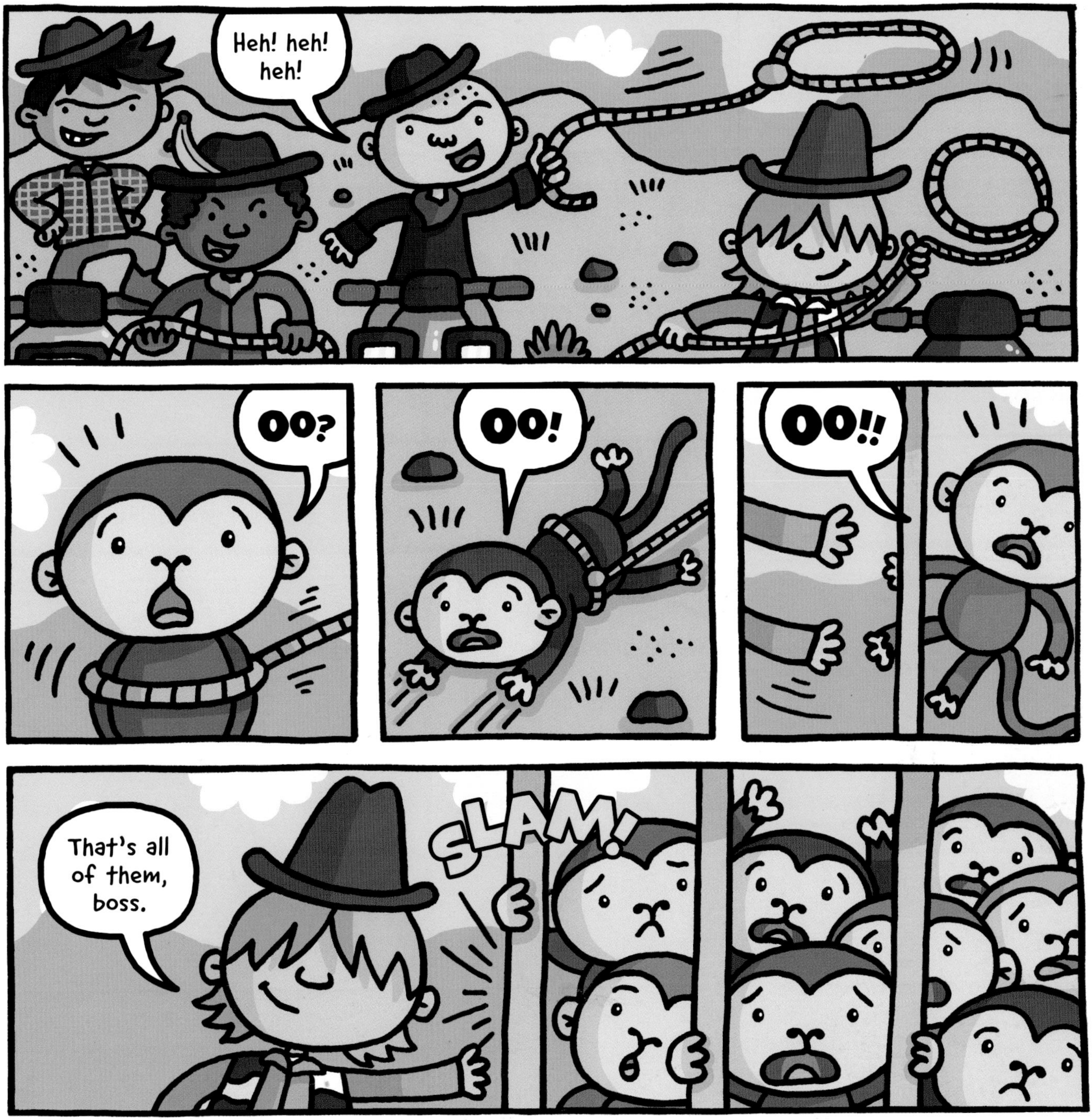
Heh! heh! heh!
OO?
OO!
OO!!
That's all of them, boss.
SLAM!

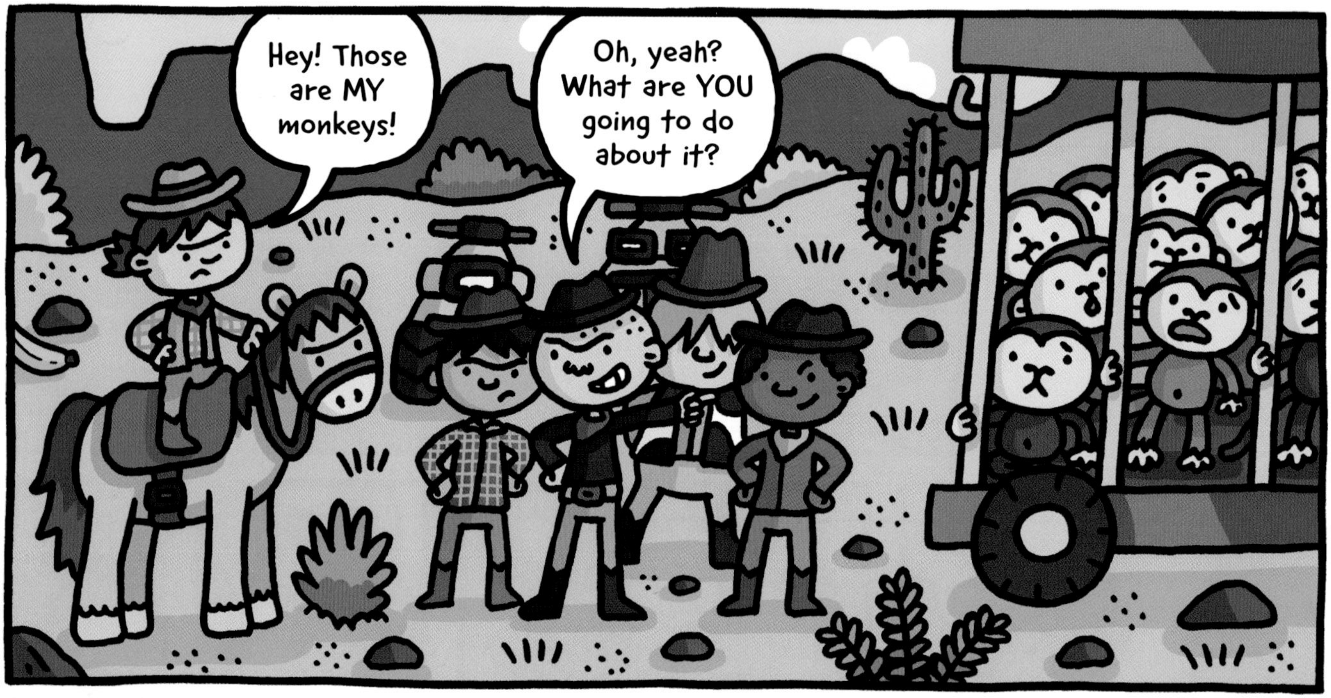
Hey! Those are MY monkeys!
Oh, yeah? What are YOU going to do about it?

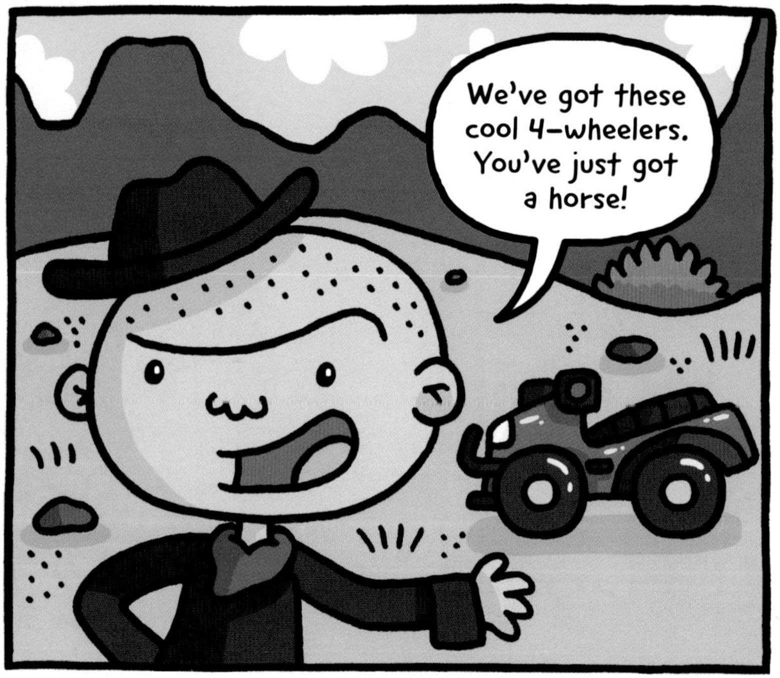
We've got these cool 4-wheelers. You've just got a horse!

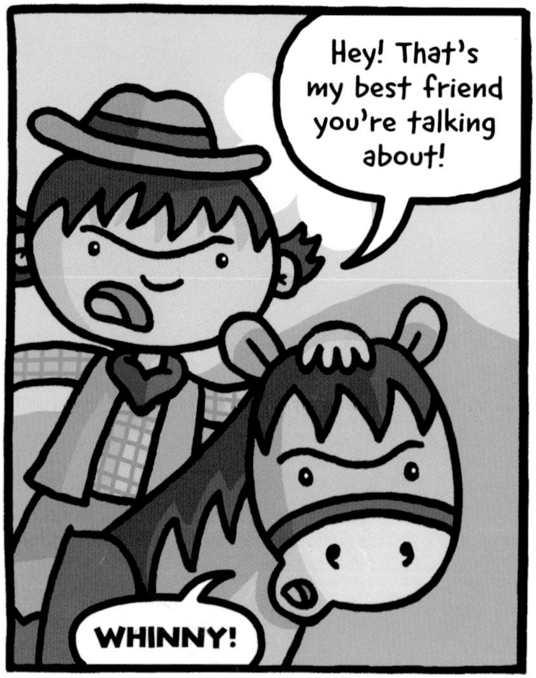
Hey! That's my best friend you're talking about!
WHINNY!

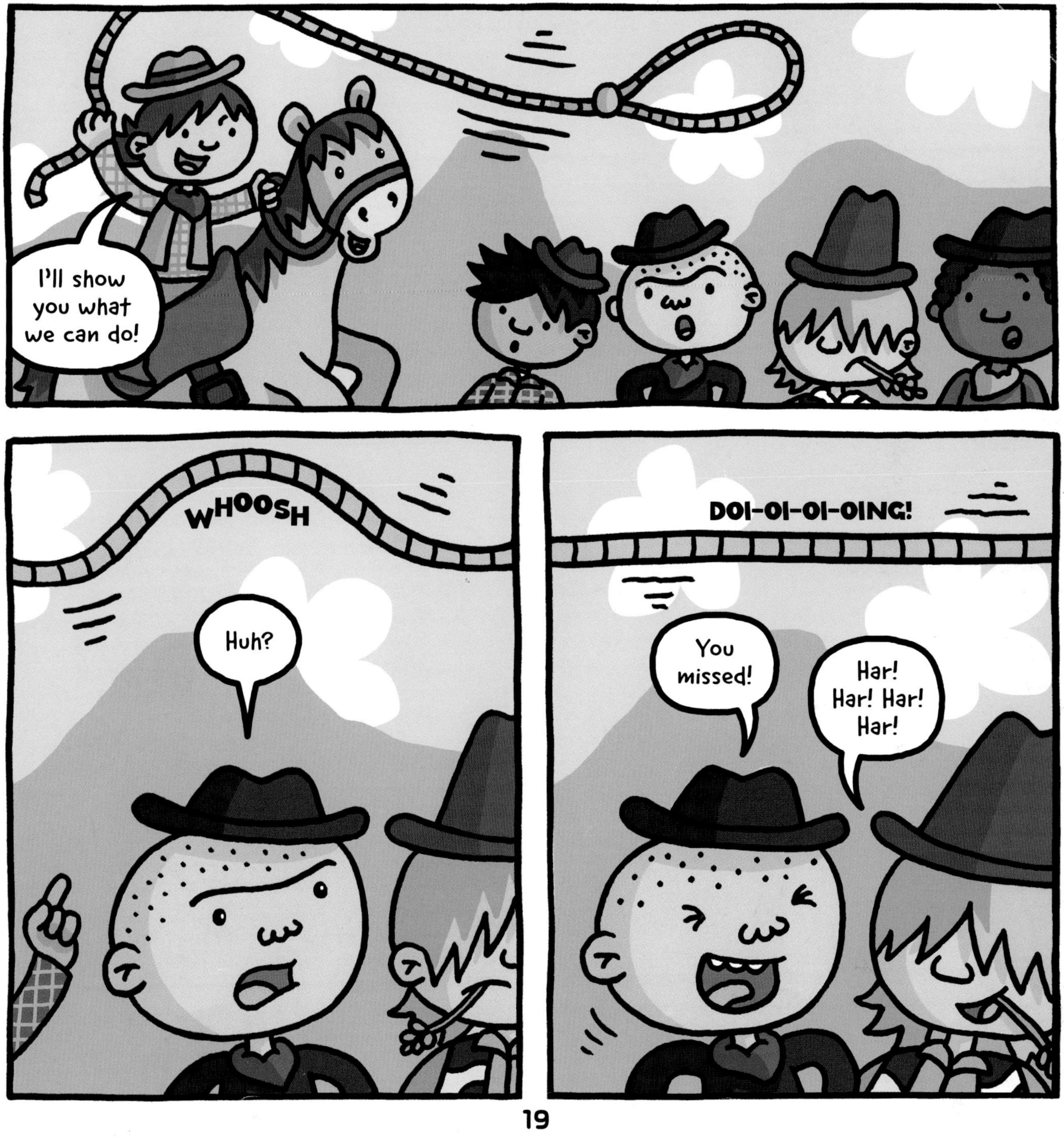

I'll show you what we can do!
WHOOSH
Huh?
DOI-OI-OI-OING!
You missed!
Har! Har! Har! Har!

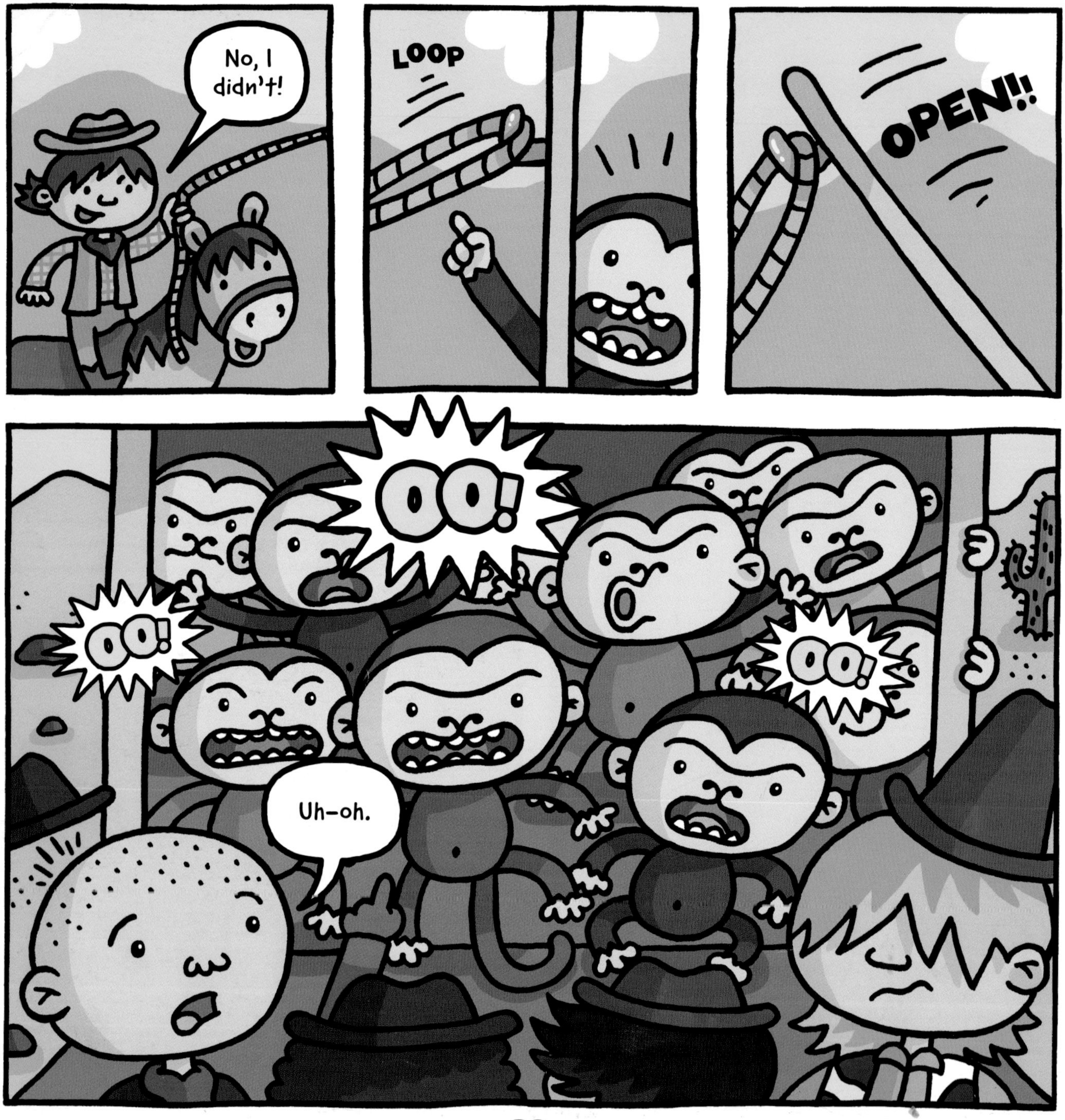
No, I didn't!
LOOP
OPEN!!
OO!
OO!
OO!
Uh-oh.

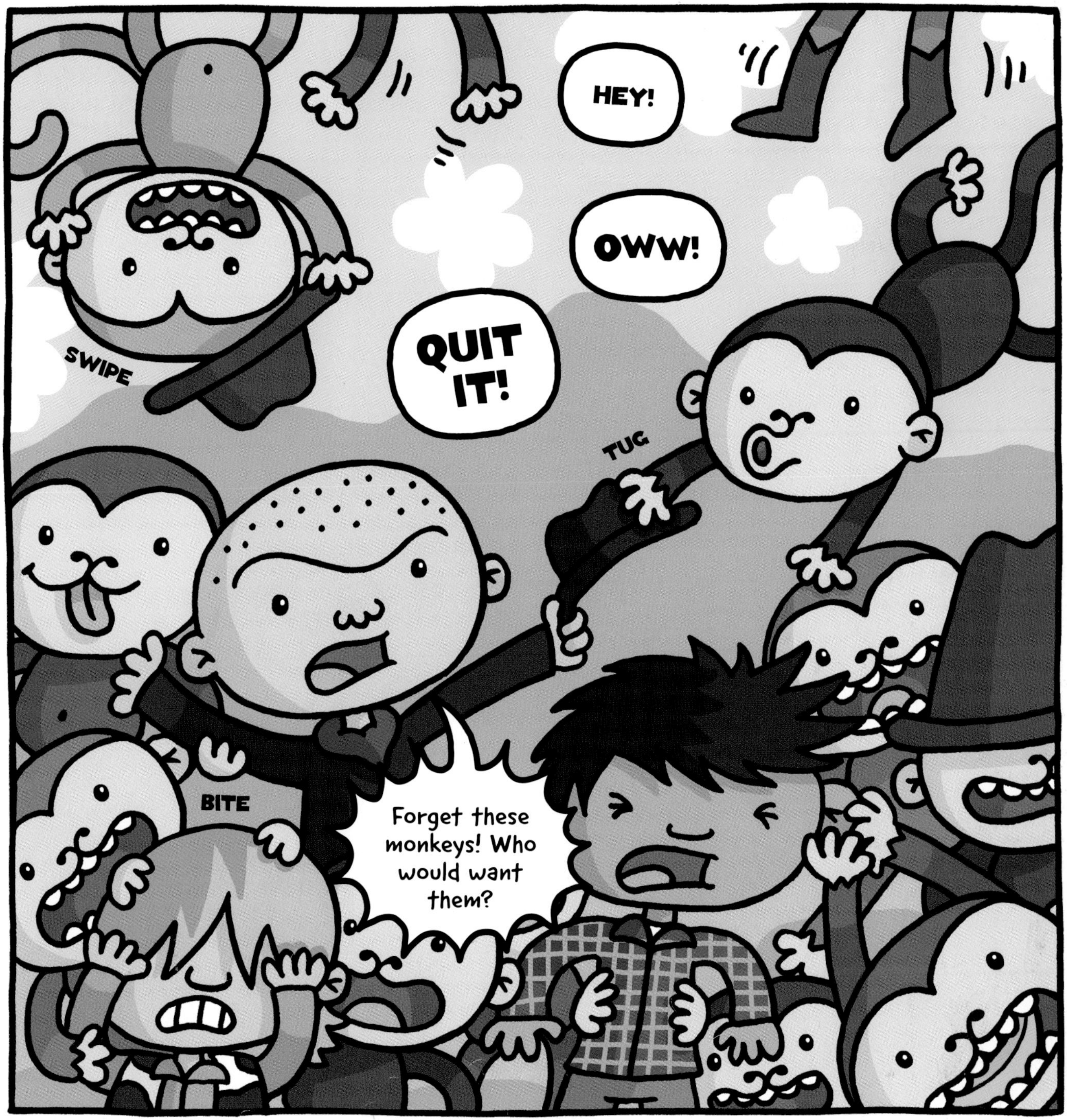
HEY!
OWW!
SWIPE
QUIT IT!
TUG
BITE
Forget these monkeys! Who would want them?

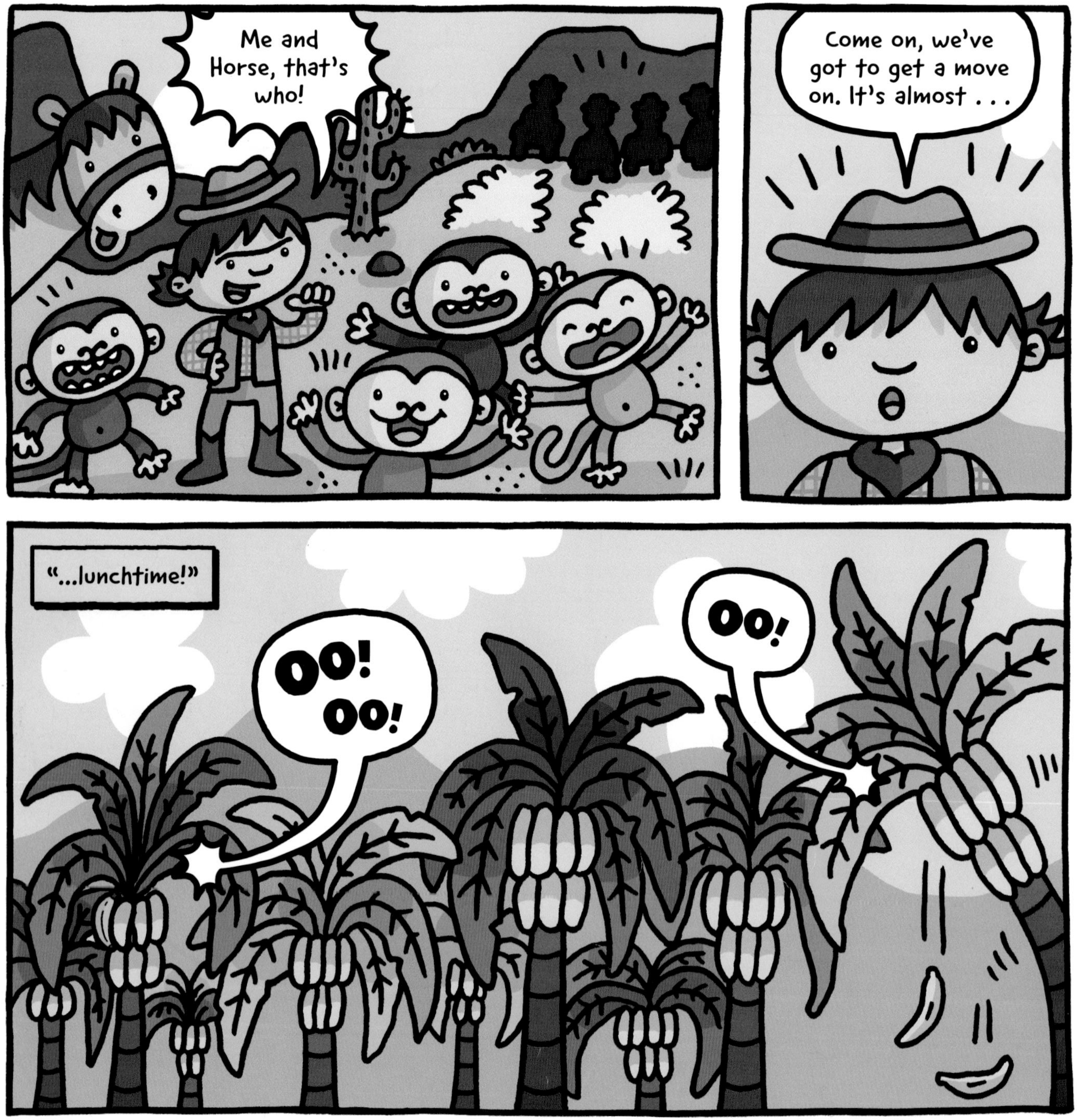
Me and Horse, that's who!
Come on, we've got to get a move on. It's almost . . .
"...lunchtime!"
OO! OO!
OO!

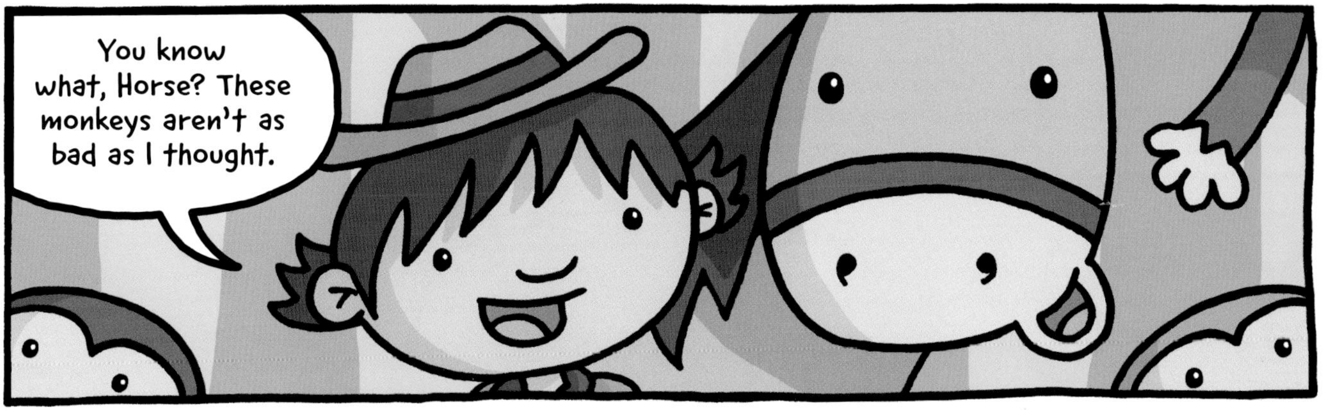
You know what, Horse? These monkeys aren't as bad as I thought.

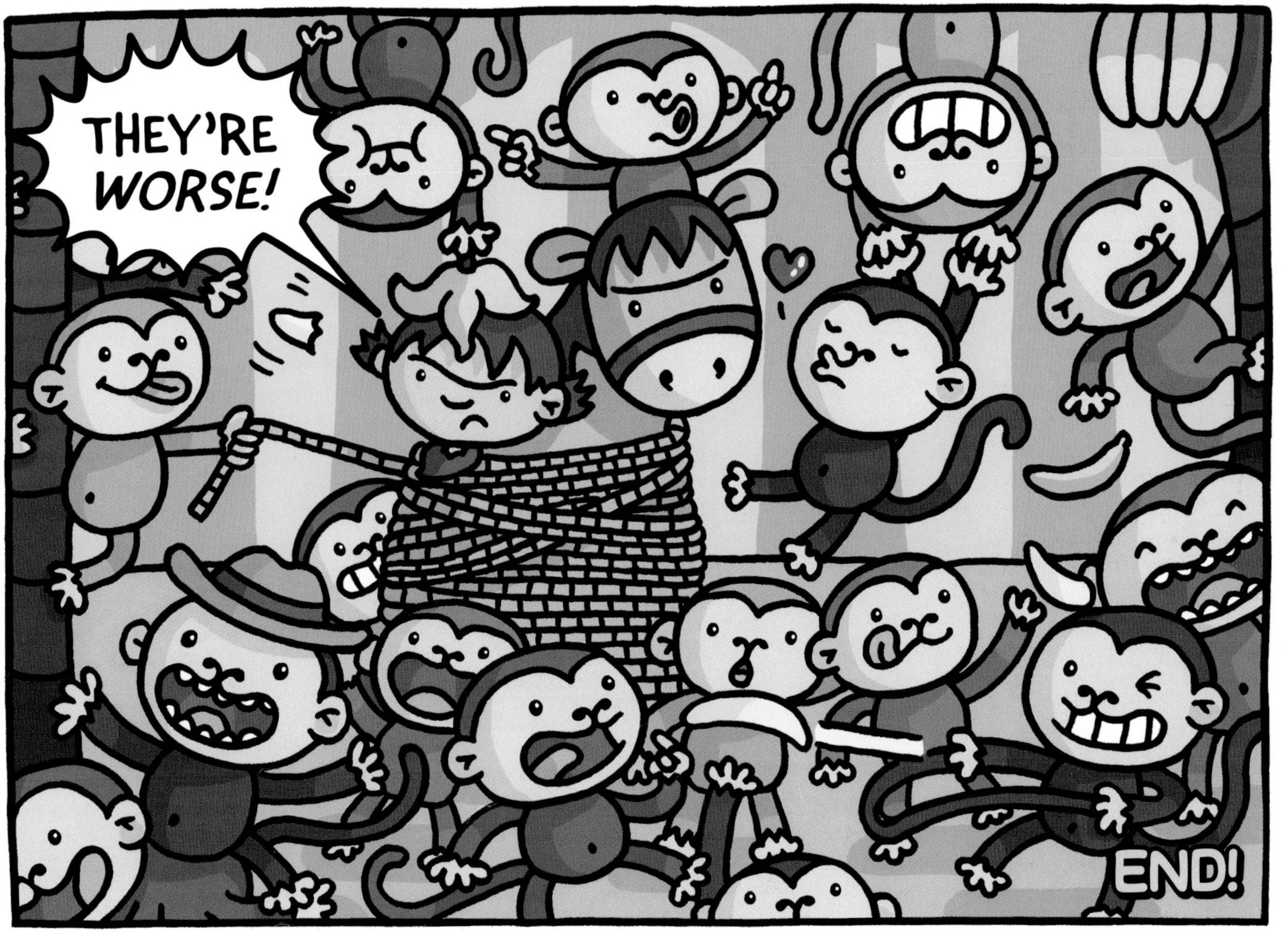
THEY'RE *WORSE!*
END!

Elsewhere in COMICS LAND...

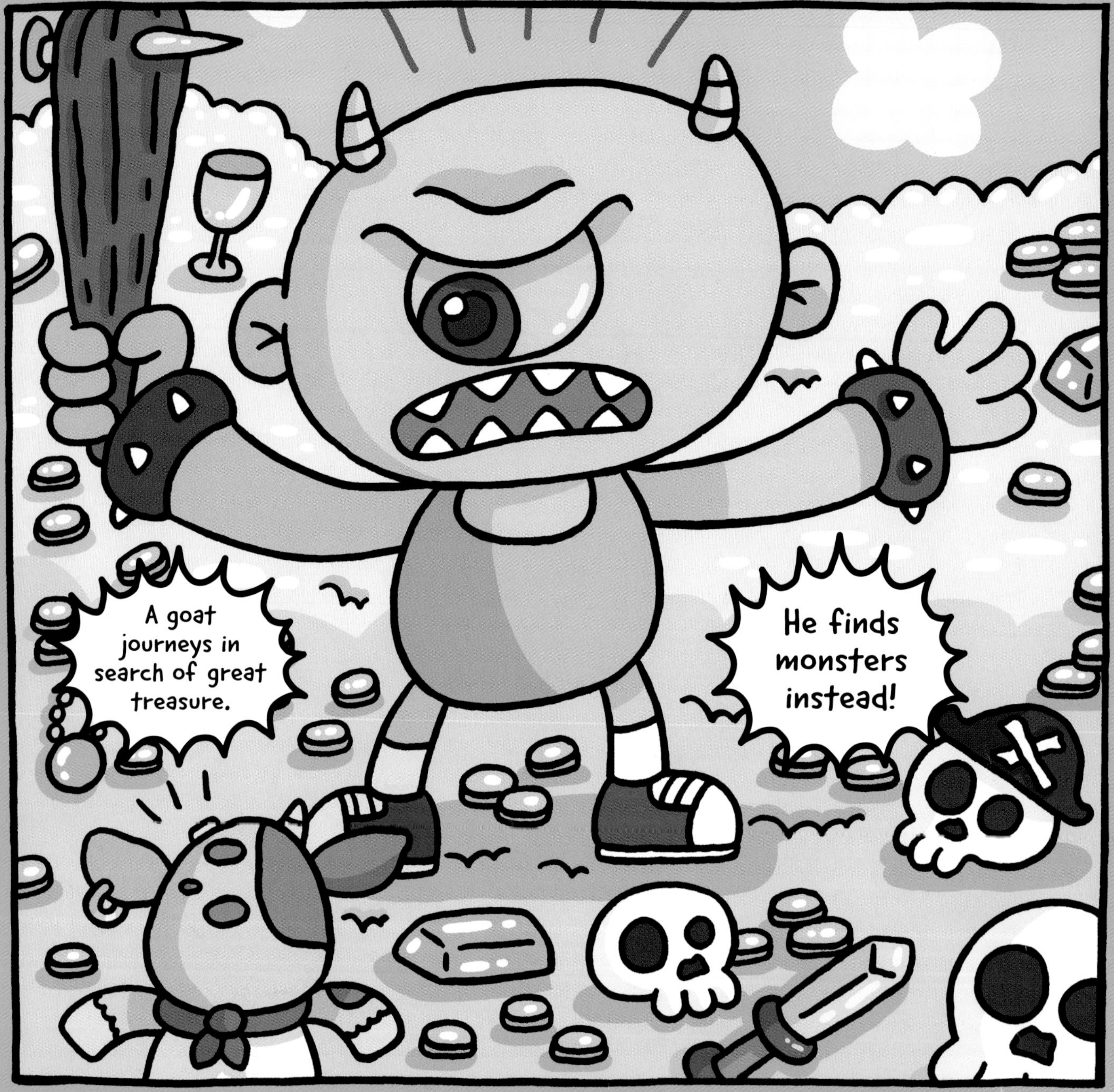
A goat journeys in search of great treasure.
He finds monsters instead!

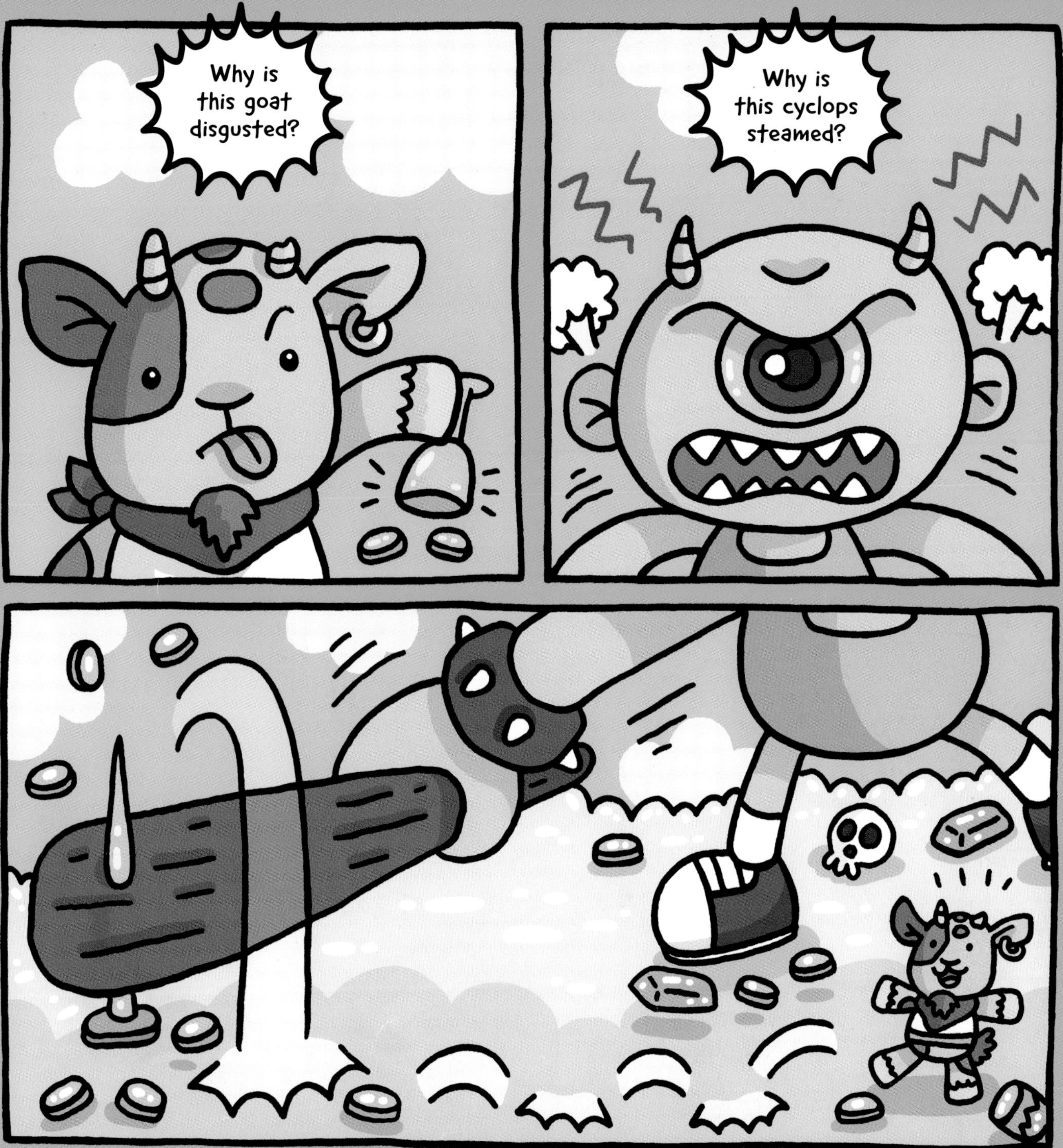
Why is this goat disgusted?
Why is this cyclops steamed?

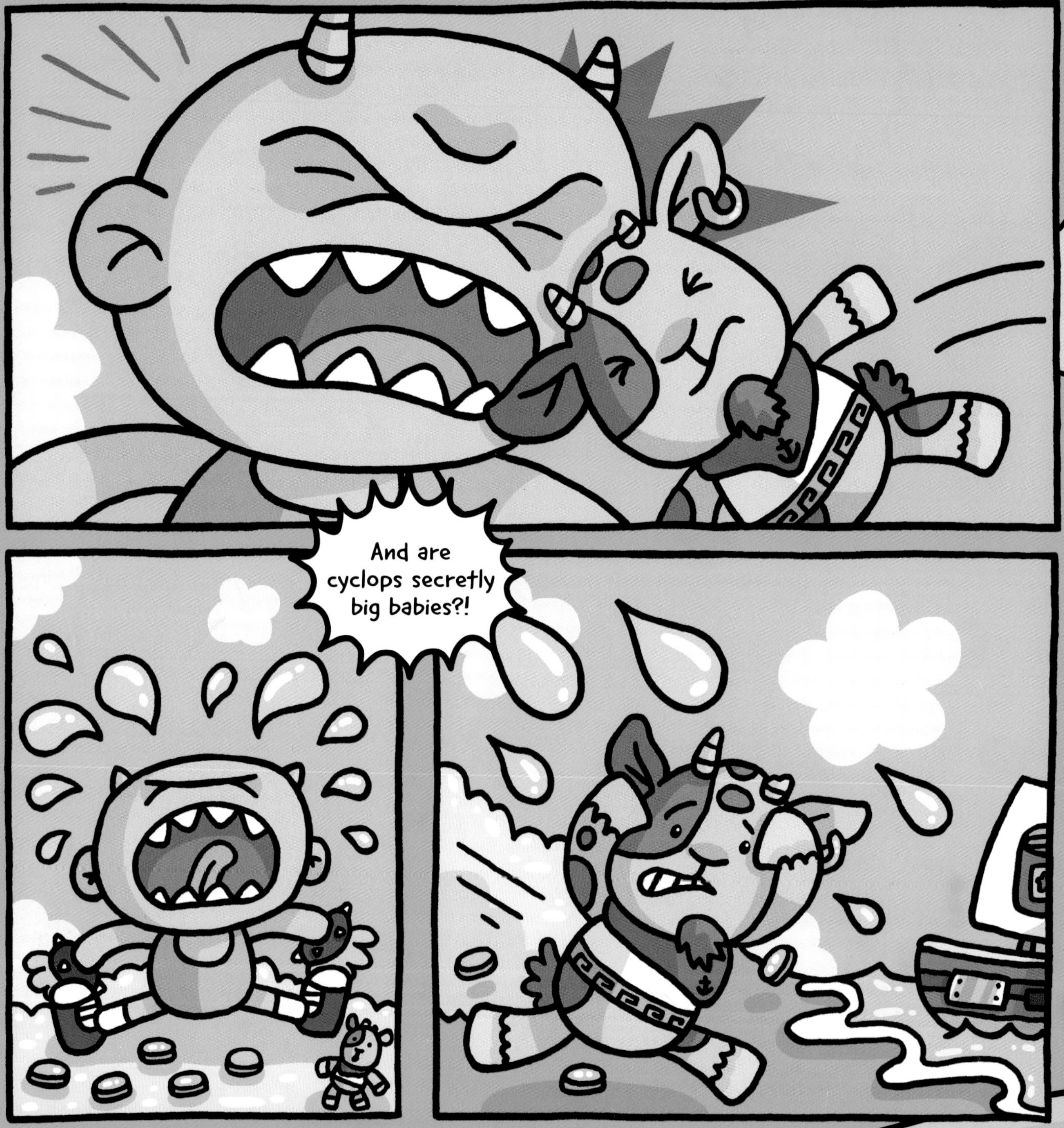
And are
cyclops secretly
big babies?!

Find out in the pages of...

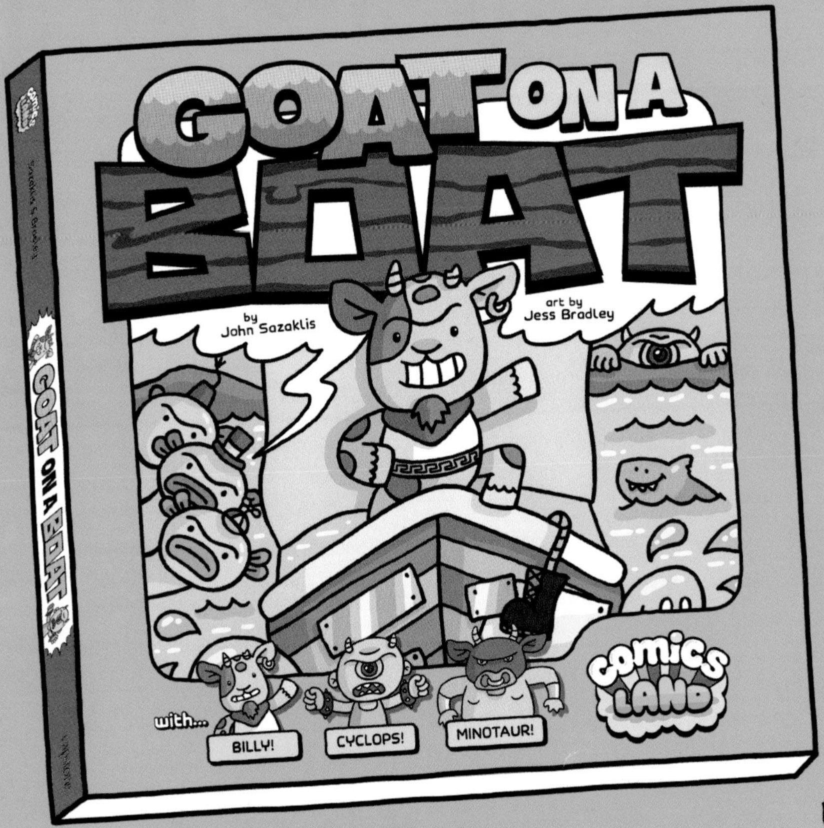

GOAT ON A BOAT
by John Sazaklis
art by Jess Bradley
with...
BILLY!
CYCLOPS!
MINOTAUR!
COMICS LAND

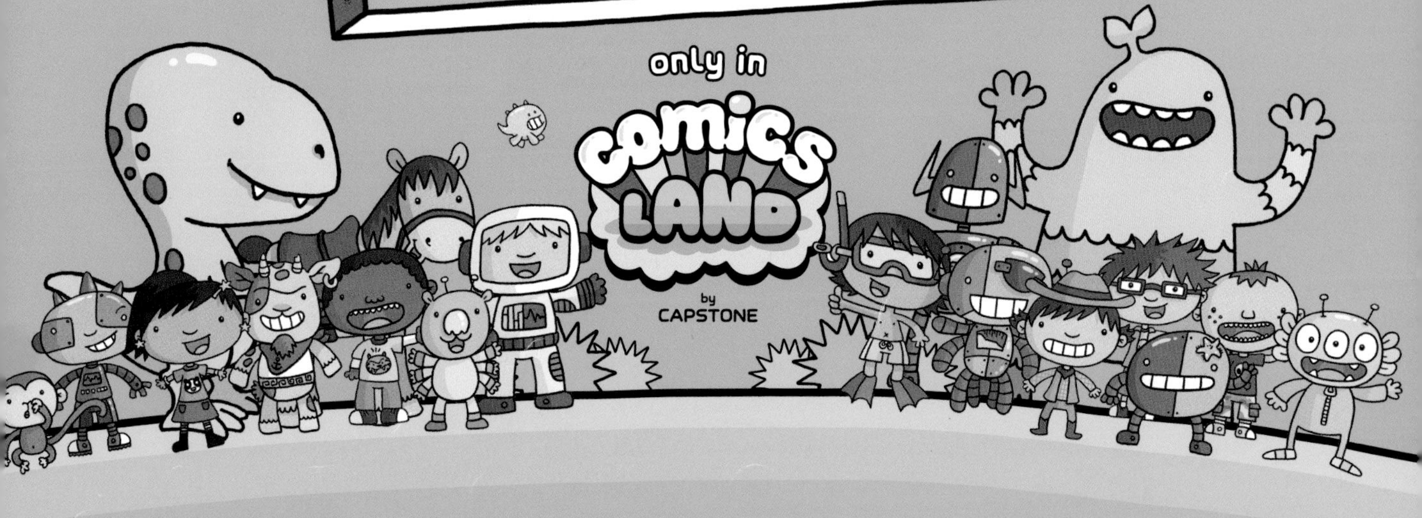

only in
COMICS LAND
by
CAPSTONE

THE GOOD, THE BAD, AND THE MONKEYS

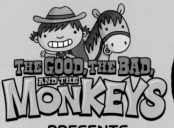

PRESENTS

GAME TIME!

Every box, balloon, and burst in a comic has a special name and job. Can you match the object with its name?

A. SOUND BURST

B. SURPRISE LINES

C. EXCITEMENT BALLOON

D. WORD BALLOON

E. MOTION LINES

F. SOUND EFFECT

G. NARRATIVE BOX

H. THOUGHT BALLOON

1=D, 2=H, 3=G, 4=A, 5=E, 6=B, 7=F, 8=C

1

2

3

4

5

6

7

POW!

8

!

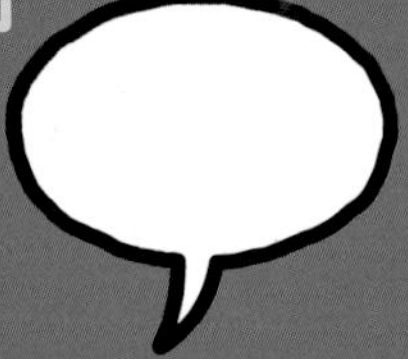

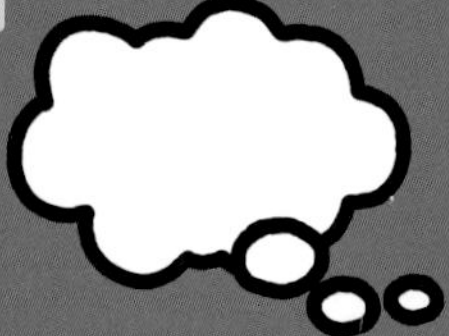

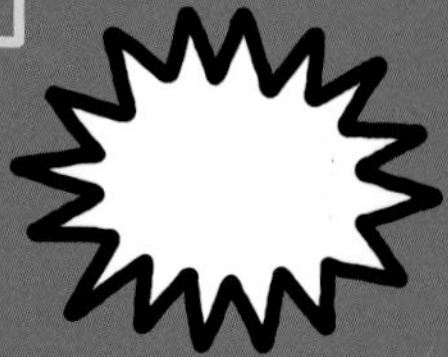

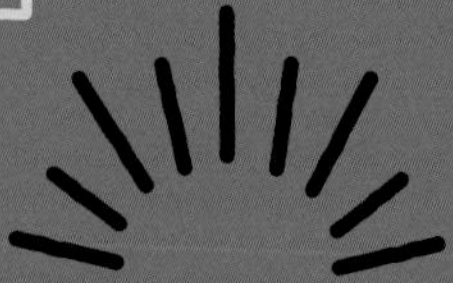

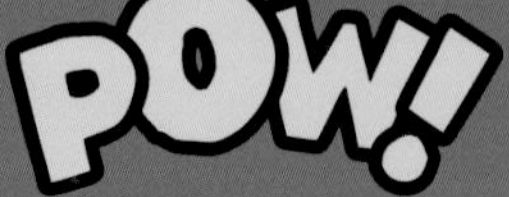

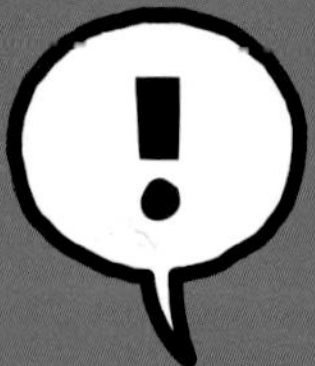

Unscramble the letters to reveal words from the story.

1. SHORE	5. YMSEKNO
2. RHED	6. BOOCWY
3. ABNNAA	7. LESTURRS
4. VORGE	8. NAIZGGR

1. HORSE, 2. HERD, 3. BANANA, 4. GROVE, 5. MONKEYS, 6. COWBOY, 7. RUSTLERS, 8. GRAZING

FIND THE BANANAS!

The wild monkeys in this story will slow down for just one thing: BANANAS! Go back and take another look at the story to find 12 green bananas.

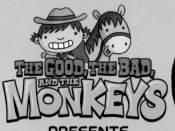

THE GOOD, THE BAD, AND THE MONKEYS

PRESENTS

DRAW COMICS!

Want to make your own comic about Jake's herd? Start by learning to draw one of the wild monkeys. Comics Land artist Jess Bradley shows you how in six easy steps!

You will need:

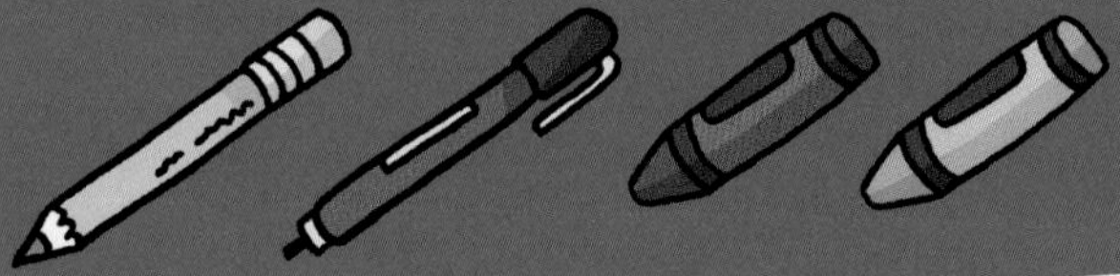

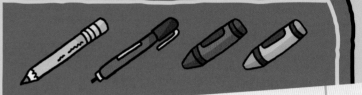

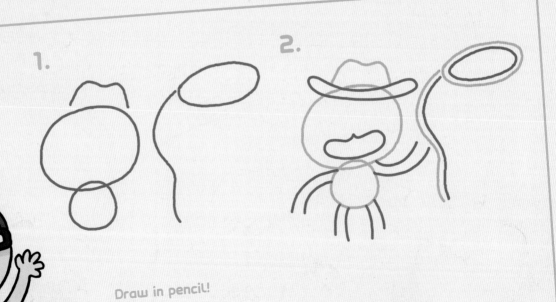

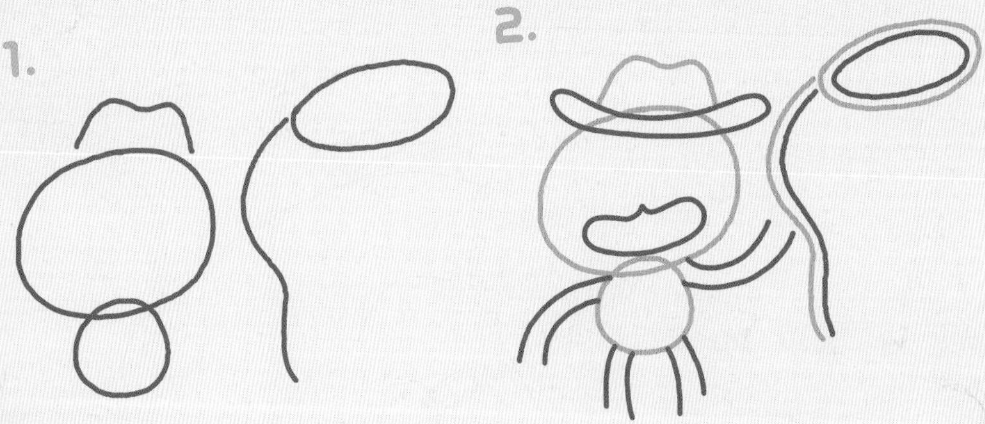
1.
2.

Draw in pencil!

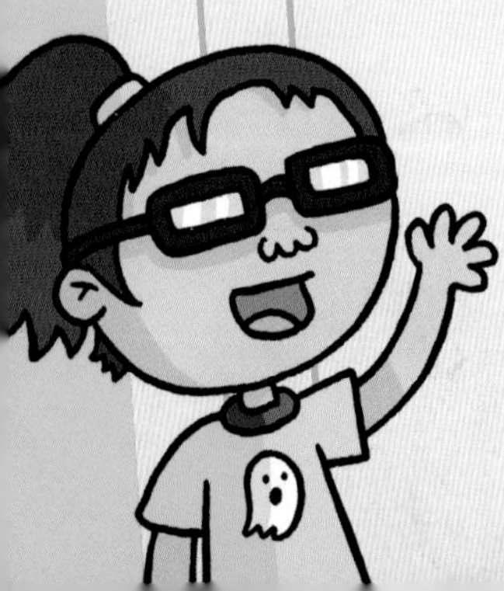

3.

4.

5.

Outline in ink!

6.

Color!

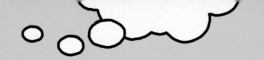

SCOTT SONNEBORN

AUTHOR

Scott Sonneborn has written 20 books, one circus (for Ringling Bros. Barnum & Bailey), and a bunch of TV shows. He's been nominated for one Emmy and spent three very cool years working at DC Comics. He lives in Los Angeles with his wife and their two sons.

JESS BRADLEY

ARTIST

Jess Bradley is an illustrator living and working in Bristol, England. She likes playing video games, painting, and watching bad films. Jess can also be heard to make a high-pitched "squeeeee" when excited, usually while watching videos clips of otters or getting new comics in the mail.

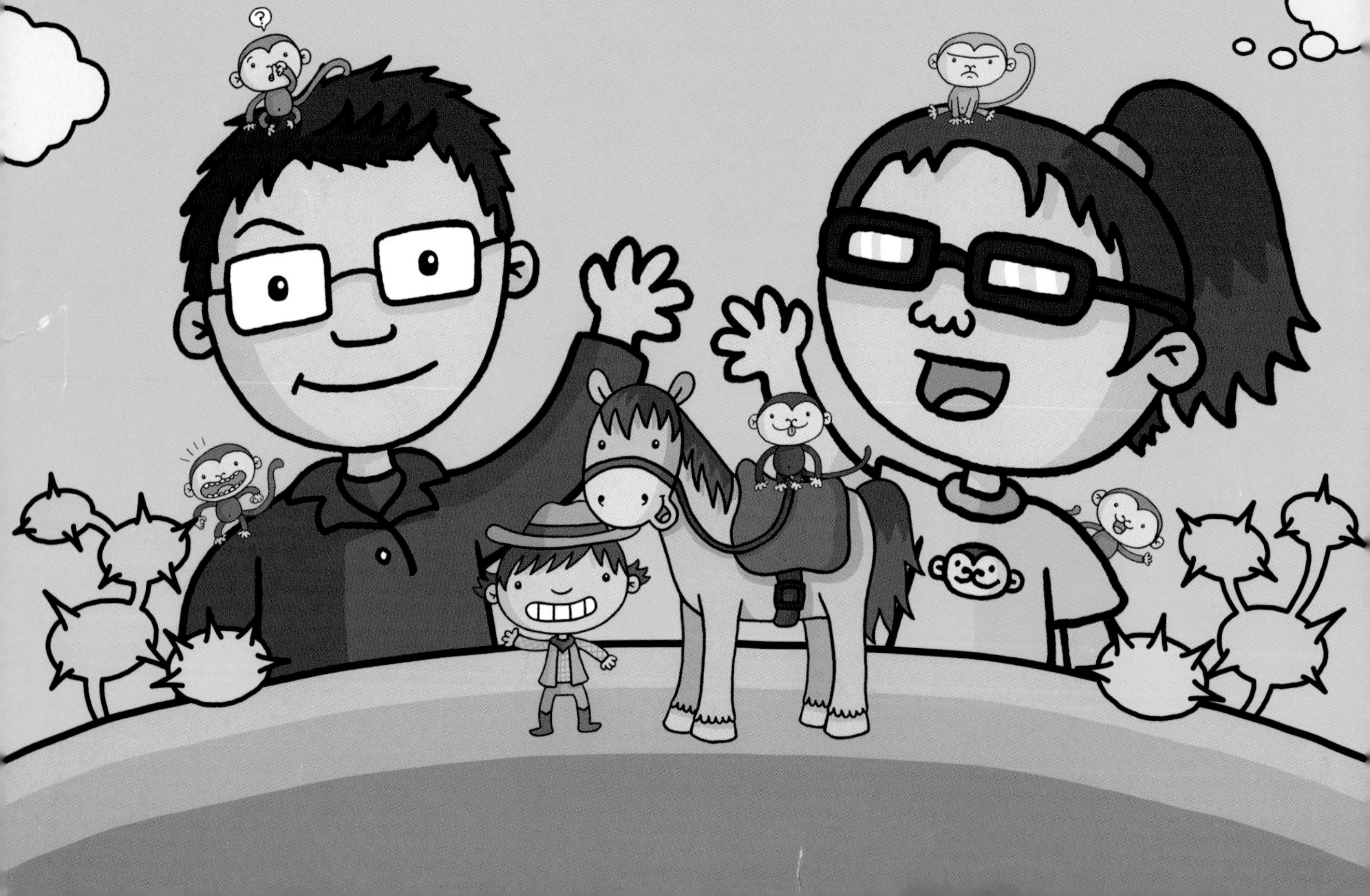
?

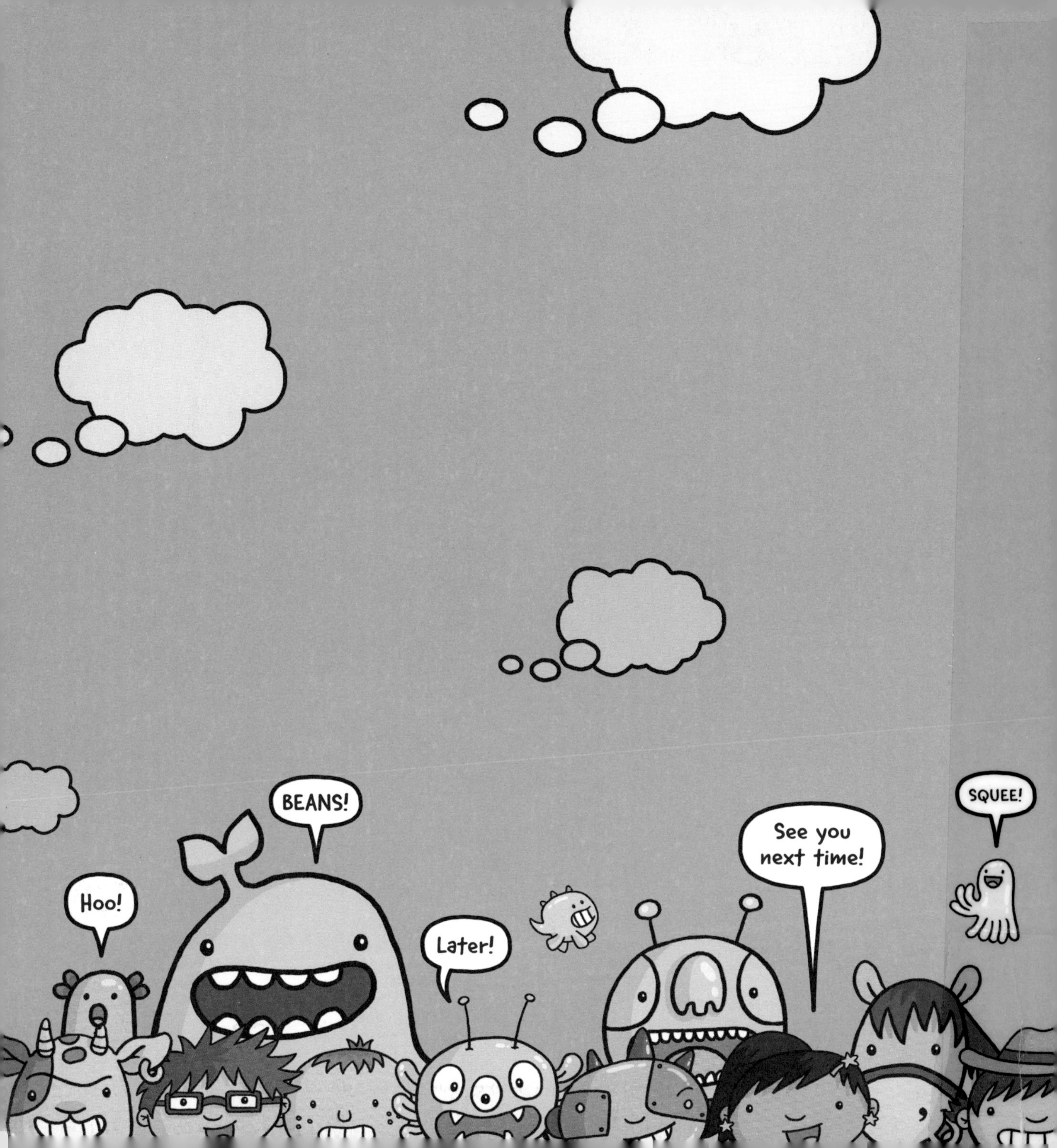
Hoo!
BEANS!
Later!
See you next time!
SQUEE!